Caper Finds a Treasure

A Tiny House Mystery, Book Seven
By Cynthia Hickey

DEDICATION

To all the victims of sex trafficking. May you find your freedom.

Chapter One

CJ did a twirl in front of the mirror in her tiny house. She'd borrowed the mirror from Mags and propped it against the wall. The full-skirted wedding dress billowed out around her. She felt like a princess.

"I have a question that's been nagging me for a while now," Mags said. "Oh, you look beautiful by the way."

"Thank you. So do you." She did, too. Mags looked quite lovely in her purple flowing gown. CJ stopped twirling and wondered when her friend was going to marry Uncle Larry. "What is it?"

"Why did Eric propose twice? Didn't you say yes the first time?" She raised her eyebrows.

"Of course, I did. He said he wanted to make sure I meant it and didn't say just yes because we were jumping off a cliff running from those bad guys at the time." She grinned. "Sometimes, my brave park ranger is a little insecure."

"Well, you are a flighty little thing."

"I am not. I'm as steadfast as they come."

She shrugged. "Does this mean you'll stop solving local mysteries?"

"Most definitely."

Mags's face fell. She did enjoy the excitement of a good mystery even if it involved near death. "I suppose you'll want children now. Noisy things that they are. I'll have to find another way to inject adventure into my life."

"Of course. Eric is already making plans to combine our tiny houses into one small house." I couldn't wait.

Uncle Larry, Mags's boyfriend and my only living relative, entered the room. "Gorgeous." He kissed my cheek and handed me a jeweler's box. "A gift from your soon-to-be husband."

I opened the box to reveal a diamond tennis bracelet. "It's beautiful."

"Make sure you keep it away from that diamond-loving dog of yours." He grinned.

"Oh, I will." I held out my hand so he could place the bracelet on my wrist. Caper, the dog I'd inherited from my grandmother, did love her diamonds. "Thank you for watching the dogs and cat for us while we're gone."

"Not a problem. Ready?" Uncle Larry crooked his arm as Mags handed me a bouquet of purple roses and baby's breath, taking the smaller one for herself. "You've an anxious groom waiting by the lake. The whole community is there, plus some curious campers."

Excitement over sharing my special day with so

many people put a bounce in my step. I couldn't wait to lay eyes on my handsome groom and board our flight to Hawaii for our honeymoon.

Mags, acting as matron of honor, stepped from the house first. When the door opened, I heard the first recorded notes of the "Wedding March." My heart threatened to beat free. My breath came in pants.

"Don't pass out on me." Uncle Larry patted my hand. "Breathe nice and slow. This is a good day. The sun is shining, God is looking down from Heaven, and you're marrying the man of your dreams."

He was right. It was a glorious day. My breathing returned to normal, and I stepped into the bright sunshine of an early spring day and took my seat in the golf cart.

A white carpet runner paved the way to the glass cathedral in the trees I'd spent so many hours renovating. An arch overflowing with purple roses and white streamers outlined Eric's form in front of the simple wooden podium. The guests stood, blocking him from my view. No matter. Good things were worth waiting for.

Smiles and claps greeted me as I moved slowly to the end of the rows of white folding chairs, finally laying eyes on Eric. Handsome in a black tux, his smile rivaled mine. Detective Davis acted as best man. Sitting calmly next to him was Caper and Eric's lab, Hershey. The day wouldn't be complete without them.

Uncle Larry placed my hand in Eric's, then took a seat in the front row. I no longer had eyes for anyone or anything but the man I was about to marry.

Eric leaned forward, his breath tickling the tendrils curled along my neck. "You're the most beautiful woman I've ever seen."

My face flushed. "You don't look so bad yourself." I couldn't believe we were finally getting married. We turned to face the preacher.

"Clarice Josephine Turley, do you…"

I must have responded correctly when prompted, but I don't remember much of the ceremony. My gaze never left Eric's face, though.

~

The next morning, I changed into a white and purple sundress and hurried back outside to meet Eric by the car. Our honeymoon was upon us.

In the car, he leaned over and kissed me. "Hello, wife."

"Hello, husband." I grinned so wide it hurt my cheeks. "Maui awaits."

He chuckled and drove us to the airport. "I've some rough drawings of my idea for our house in the glove compartment if you'd like to take a look. Our house will be about five-hundred square feet."

"Positively huge." I laughed, pulling a large sheet of paper from the glove compartment. "Bigger kitchen, bigger living space, two bathrooms, and two bedrooms. We'll be positively spoiled with all that space."

He gripped my hand. "That second bedroom will come in handy when we have a child."

My face heated. "Yes, it will."

A two-hour flight to Dallas, then another eight hours to the mainland, before taking a smaller plane to Maui left me with a lot of time to dream of our future. I stepped off the plane, fully rested, to be greeted by a woman with shiny dark hair.

"Aloha." She smiled and draped the fragrant lei around my neck, then did the same for Eric. "Enjoy your honeymoon, courtesy of your uncle." She handed me a letter.

Bless him. He'd paid for the entire hotel bill for the week of our stay as a wedding gift. Since he owned the tiny house community and the land the campground sat on, I guess he could afford it. "Did you know about this, Eric?"

"No, but it doesn't surprise me. You're a very beloved niece." He took my hand and led me to the waiting jeep that would take us to our hotel on the beach.

A small tropical hut with all the modern conveniences would be our home for the next five days. Waiting for us inside was a welcome basket of fruit and champagne on ice.

"What do you want to do first?" Eric poured us both a flute. "To us." He raised his in a toast.

"To us." Let's sit on the porch, I mean lanai, and watch the water for a while."

"Sounds perfect."

We sat in white wicker chairs and watched as windsurfers skimmed across the waves. Their sails dotted the ocean with every color of the rainbow. Families strolled along the shore looking for shells. An old woman in a peaked cap picked up seaweed while a man in a matching hat skimmed a box across the water's surface looking for flounder. Other than the mountain lake I lived by, I'd never seen a more idyllic sight. I couldn't wait to see the sunset over this same stretch of beach.

I glanced to the hut next to us. A pretty young girl with a sad look on her face leaned on a railing draped with beach towels. When she caught my glance, she ducked back inside, pulling a silk kimono tight around her. Even in paradise, a teen girl could be moody. Shrugging, I sipped my drink and watched the happy vacationers.

A man's loud voice boomed from next door, right before the young girl darted back outside and raced for the beach. The man, most likely her father, ordered her to come back. The girl kept running.

I set my glass on a table next to my chair and stood.

"Stay out of it, sweetheart. Unless he turns violent, we pretend nothing is happening."

"You're right." I sat back down, determined not to let anything ruin our honeymoon. "She just looks so sad."

"A family squabble." He pulled me close for a kiss. "I'll never get tired of the feel of your lips against mine."

"Honeymoon?" The man next door asked.

"Yes." Eric lifted his head and smiled.

"I remember mine. We went to Greece. Best week of my life. Name's Joe Landon."

"Eric and CJ Drake."

How I loved the sound of that. I smiled a greeting and turned my attention to where the young girl sat on the sand near the water. "Teenagers, right?"

Joe laughed. "Yes, this one is quite strong-willed. Lacey!"

She glanced over her shoulder and slowly returned to the hut. Without a word, she stepped inside, her long blonde hair hiding her face.

"You look familiar, Mrs. Drake." His eyes narrowed. "Have you been on television or in the newspaper?"

"A bit." I didn't elaborate. He either knew I was the nosy one of the Ozarks, as some called me, or he didn't

"Enjoy your stay, folks." Joe followed her inside.

"I wonder where the wife is," I said. "Isn't it strange that she didn't come out when her daughter took off?"

"Don't make a mystery out of nothing. You promised."

I nodded. What I promised was not to get involved in any more crimes. I didn't say anything about helping a girl in trouble. But, since I didn't see any bruises or other evidence of abuse, Eric was right. It was none of my business.

Later that evening, I changed into a bright yellow sundress and matching sandals, then strolled with my new husband to a small outdoor diner for supper. A waitress in a grass skirt and bathing suit top handed us menus.

"Oh, the mango salmon sounds delicious," I said. "I'll have that."

Eric ordered the same. "I'm looking forward to snorkeling tomorrow. I saw the perfect spot right off our beach. When the tide goes out, the pool is surrounded by coral."

"Good." I'd mentioned to him my fear of sharks and barracudas, a warning mentioned on the paper we signed in order to rent snorkeling equipment. "Do you still want to go to Molokai Island?"

"One of the days we're here." He laughed. "Don't worry. I won't let anything eat you."

"I know I'm being silly, but…" I glanced up in time to see Joe usher Lacey into a waiting SUV.

The girl's eyes widened. Was it my imagination or did her lips form the words "Help me," as she was shoved inside?

Chapter Two

I couldn't get the look of Lacey's pleading face out of my mind and woke the next morning with gritty eyes from lack of sleep. My morning person of a husband—I'd discovered during the times he slept on my sofa in the past to protect me—had coffee and a smile waiting for me on the lanai.

"Good morning, beautiful."

I mumbled some type of response. Without coffee, I was barely coherent.

"It looks as if our neighbors have checked out." He motioned to the hut next door.

The towels were gone from the railing and the window curtains open. "I'm worried about the girl." I told him of her plea for help.

"Are you sure?" His brow furrowed.

"Well, not exactly." It could have been my imagination. I did watch way too many true crime shows on television.

He laid a hand on my arm. "Relax. We're on our honeymoon. Would it relieve your mind to watch the news tonight and see whether anything is going on?"

"Yes." I smiled.

"You know we can't do anything if there is."

I nodded. Getting involved with something in an unfamiliar place would be a lot different than doing so at home where I knew the grounds and Eric knew the mountain.

"I've had enough almost getting killed to last a lifetime," he said, smiling to take the sting from his words.

I agreed and shoved Lacey's face from my mind. "It's time to settle down to a normal married life."

He laughed. "If only I could believe that. You crave adventure as much as Mags does."

"No, I don't." I frowned.

"Keep telling yourself that."

Did I? Had my sheltered childhood and the years of caring for an ailing grandmother led me to wanting the exact opposite I'd had in the past? What kind of a mother would that make me? I'd put any children I had in danger. I vowed right then not to get involved in anymore mysteries no matter how much the desire tugged at me.

After breakfast we suited up and headed for the tide pool near our hotel. I put my mask and snorkel into place, looped the waterproof camera around my wrist, and stretched out on my stomach, floating weightlessly in the water.

So many different types of fishes. One needle-nosed one came close enough to tap my mask. I chuckled, which sounded more like a gurgle, and followed my little silvery friend. He didn't care for the company and whipped around and came at me so fast my arms windmilled in an attempt to propel me backward.

I got the hint. Observe only, no interaction. I snapped a picture of Erik and continued my exploration, deciding I liked snorkeling.

When my back felt sunburned, I stood and removed my mask, breathing deep of the salt air. A few natives waved from their wanderings on the beach. A tattered sofa sat under a palm tree. A place for a body to rest or someone's home? Unfortunately, even paradise had homeless people.

"Ready to hit the big water?" Eric emerged from the water.

"Sure." I felt like comfortable in the water now.

Bad idea. The water outside the tide pool was murky. The theme song from *Jaws* played in my head, and I whipped my head from side to side, hyperventilating. Where was the clear water off Maui's shore? Any ocean predator could be on me before I saw them.

A strand of seaweed tickled my arm and I screamed, swimming as fast as possible for the shore. I definitely preferred the tide pool. Once I reached the safety of the beach, I sat on the sand and wrapped my arms around my folded knees to wait for Eric. He waved from the water and dove out of sight.

A group of teenage girls passed in front of me, clearly part of a youth group, considering the two adult women who trailed behind them. The girls giggled and stared as a young man with a chiseled chest and low-slung swimming trunks strolled past.

He tossed his long, dark hair out of his eyes, said, "Aloha," and continued on his way.

The girls turned and followed, still giggling.

I couldn't ever remember acting like that, but then I'd stayed pretty much to myself at their age.

My husband finally emerged from the water, grinning and sunburned. "Why'd you get out?"

"Sharks and barracudas." I shrugged.

He laughed and kissed me. "Come on. Let's go rest a bit before the luau. I won't even care if you ogle the male dancers."

"Because you'll be doing the same with the females." I hugged his arm and leaned my cheek against him. He smelled like salt and suntan lotion.

After a nap and other afternoon delights, we woke and got ready for our evening of fun. Hand in hand, we moved up the beach to a larger hotel where the luau would be held.

Large tables and smaller intimate ones faced a makeshift platform a few inches off the sand. Off to one side, a pig roasted on a spit, filling the evening air with the delicious aroma of dinner.

Eric pulled out a chair for me at one of the smaller tables. A few tables over was the crowd of youth I'd observed following after the handsome local. Squeals filled the air as he stepped onto the stage with a tropical-patterned scarf wrapped around his lower half. His skin glistened with oil.

Soon, two other men joined him, and the trio put on a show of fire breathing that left me breathless. Their act was followed by hula dancers.

A server brought us Hawaiian drinks in cups made to look like coconuts, complete with tiny umbrellas. I took a sip and wrinkled my nose. Too strong.

Eric ordered me another without the alcohol. "Would you prefer wine?"

"No, I want something that tastes tropical without the strong alcohol taste." I smiled. "Thank you."

"I'd prefer a beer." He winked. "But I also want to drink something tropical while in Maui."

Uh-oh. I caught sight of one of the girls wandering toward the hotel after Mr. Hot Dancer Dude. It didn't take but a second for one of the chaperones to follow, returning shortly after with a disappointed young lady in tow.

"Oh, to be young again," I said, sounding very much like Mags.

"I thought you didn't date much." Eric's mouth crooked.

"I didn't, but I did have my share of crushes. Just never acted on any of them. Turns out I didn't need to. Life brought me you."

He leaned close. "I love you."

"Ditto." I raised my face for a kiss.

When I pulled back, I caught sight of the young man the girls chased speaking with Joe Landon. The older man glanced my way, scowled, and led the other one out of sight. I got the impression he knew exactly who I was and why I'd been in the news. A shudder skittered down my spine.

"You cold?" Eric asked.

"No." I forced a smile, hoping my presence hadn't brought trouble to paradise. I did tend to do that on more than one occasion. Trouble followed me like a kid to an ice cream truck. I didn't want anything to mar my honeymoon. "I thought the

Landons checked out. I just saw Joe talking with one of the dancers."

"Maybe they simply chose a hotel somewhere else. How about a moonlight stroll after that delicious dinner?" Eric stood and held out his hand.

"That sounds wonderful." I slipped off my sandals and dangled them from the fingers of my free hand. The damp sand at the water's edge felt cool on my feet. The sound of the waves kissing the shore erased my feelings of unease. I was most likely looking for trouble where none existed. "It's been a good day."

"Perfect." Eric smiled. "Maybe we should sell everything we have and move here."

"Silly. You love the mountain and the lake too much to ever leave. So do I, but we can come back here someday."

"How about our fiftieth anniversary? We can see other places in the world until then."

"That sounds wonderful."

The next morning, we woke early to take the drive to Hana. Relieved Eric was driving the treacherous road, I clicked on my seatbelt in the convertible we'd rented. "Try not to drive over a cliff."

"I'll do my best." He laughed and drove away from our hut.

The scenery was idyllic. Sheer cliffs on our left fell to the ocean. Jungle covered the hills to the right. Things got hairy when a car came from the other direction, but Eric hugged the right side as close as possible, grinning. He was enjoying the danger.

Leaving the driving up to him, I snapped photos,

wanting to capture every bit of the beauty surrounding us. In my rearview mirror, I spotted a vehicle coming up fast. Too fast for a road like the one we were on. "Uh, Eric."

He glanced in the rearview mirror. "What are they? Idiots?"

"Pull over and let them pass."

"There's nowhere to pull over. Not here anyway." He pressed the accelerator.

My heart lodged in my throat as I clutched the door handle. The car behind us was right on our bumper.

Eric cut me a sideways glance. "What did you do?"

"Nothing."

"CJ?"

"When Landon saw me last night, he quickly ducked out of sight. I think he knows how I like to butt my nose in where it doesn't belong. That's suspicious behavior, right?"

"A little." A muscle ticked in his jaw. "I can't believe trouble with a capital T followed us here."

"Maybe it was an accident, a coincidence."

"Ha. Nothing is an accident with you, sweetheart." He pulled to the side of the road. "See if you can tell who's in the car?"

We stared as they passed us. The windows were too dark to see inside.

"Just someone with no sense of how to drive on a dangerous road," Eric said, pulling out of the ditch.

The rest of the drive to Hana went without any more scares, and we arrived at the seven pools. A rainbow arched over the falls that fell from one pool to another. I wasn't surprised to see the youth group of girls there frolicking in the water. We weren't the only ones visiting all the normal tourist attractions. I couldn't wait to see the Haleakala volcano tomorrow.

Eric and I ate a packed lunch next to the pools, and I lifted my face to the sun's rays. The perfect temperature was only marred each afternoon by a fine mist that arrived right after the sun surfers left the water off our beach. I swore we could set our watches by it, which meant the rain would arrive soon.

I wasn't disappointed. I could see the mist but with the humidity could barely feel it. If not for the way my hair frizzed, I wouldn't know it was raining. "There's that young man again. He seems to be everywhere that group of girls is." I wondered why the chaperones didn't ask him to stay away.

"Nothing strange about a young man following a group of pretty girls," Eric said. "I followed a group once that attended the same summer camp I did as a kid. It's what boys do."

I supposed. Still, something about the guy's manner seemed almost predatory.

Chapter Three

The travel brochure warned the temperature on top of the volcano would be chilly. They weren't kidding. The moment I stepped out of the car, I shivered and grabbed the sweater I'd tossed in the back seat.

The view into the crater looked like I envisioned the surface of the moon to look like. Hills and craters. A small group of hikers descended a trail to the gray sandy surface.

"Want to take that hike?" Eric asked.

I shook my head. "The view from up here is just fine." My gaze followed a duck waddling among the tourists. I'd read that particular breed could only be found on Maui.

Turning, I leaned against the railing to study the others crowding against the railing. Five days on Maui wouldn't be enough. Someday, I'd like to take a cruise that traveled among all the Hawaiian Islands. Something else to look forward to with Eric.

I'd gotten so used to seeing the youth group of

girls it seemed strange not to spot them among the crowd. I shrugged. Maybe teenagers weren't as interested in a sleeping volcano as I was.

Eric and I wandered around the area, marveling at the view of the island from that height, then climbed in the car and drove to the Twin Falls waterfall. Again, we squeezed in with the tourists to marvel over the eighty-foot high falls.

"I've had enough of crowds." Eric led me back to the car. "Let me see that travel brochure. There must be plenty of beautiful places not so crowded." He flipped through the pages. "Feel like hiking? There's a lot to see on the Pipiwai Trail, and we can go at our leisure, lingering back if too many people show up."

Glad I'd worn walking shoes, I nodded. "That's where the bamboo forest is." Which also meant another harrowing drive to Hana. I shed my sweater and climbed into the car.

Thankfully, we arrived without any scary incidents, spending the time talking about the future, combining our houses, children. Dreaming about my future with Eric might be one of the most wonderful times in my life.

We stopped at a general store in Hana and bought snacks and bottled water, along with a guide map for the trail. "Don't go swimming under the falls or in the infinity pool," the clerk warned. "If you're in the pool, and a flashflood comes, you'll be swept over the falls. Oh, and the mosquitos are terrible. It is a jungle after all." She added a can of bug spray to our purchases.

Our next stop was the national park where we

paid our fee and crossed the highway to start our hike, liberally dosed with bug spray. Normally, I wasn't a physical type of person, but there was something about hiking in paradise that spurred me on.

A few others followed the trail. Ahead a group led by a trail guide filled the air with their chatter. Eric and I held back a bit before proceeding.

"Maybe we should have gone to a deserted island." I smiled up at him.

"There are a lot of people here." He gave me a quick kiss. "We're far enough behind that it'll seem as if we're alone."

We strolled along until stopping to marvel at the 200-foot Makahiku Falls. "Wow. Each waterfall we see seems to be bigger than the last."

"It's gorgeous all right." He motioned his head to a metal bridge. "Look at that."

My heart leaped into my throat. "Uh—"

"Come on, scaredy-cat. For someone who has faced killers, you're frightened of the smallest things. They look sturdy enough. Plenty of people have crossed before us."

I glanced back, catching sight of someone coming through the foliage. If I wanted to remain alone with my husband, I'd have to keep going. Tightly gripping the railing of the bridge, I took small steps across, keeping my eyes on my feet until I bumped into Eric.

"Look down, CJ."

"No, thank you."

He laughed. "Look."

I leaned over, staring at the crevice under us. My

sunglasses slipped from my face, lost forever. My favorite pair. Sighing, I took baby steps again, leaving Eric to follow.

I stepped into the bamboo forest and stared up and up. The breeze blew the stalks together filling the air with the musical sound of a windchime. "This is marvelous." Closing my eyes, I listened, having truly stepped into God's country. I reached out to touch one of the leaves, pricking my finger.

Movement made me catch a glimpse of someone behind us, this time from off the trail. Why hadn't the person caught up to us by now? Eric and I weren't exactly rushing through the hike.

Narrowing my eyes, I stared through the stalks of bamboo. "Someone is following us," I whispered.

"Are you sure?" His gaze followed mine.

"I catch glimpses. They stay just far enough back so as not to catch up to us."

"Honeymooners like us who want to be alone?"

"No. It's only one person."

Eric's expression grew serious, and he grabbed my hand. "Let's keep going."

We made our way nimbly across a creek, hopping from rock to rock and reaching the 400-foot Waimoku Falls and the end of the trail. We waited for someone to come out of the forest. No one did, reinforcing my thought that whoever followed us didn't want to be seen.

I kept an eye peeled on the road behind us as we drove back to our hut. I couldn't shake the feeling that something bad had happened, and I was somehow involved or soon would be, whether I wanted to be or not.

"Relax." Eric pulled me over and kissed me. "Enjoy the scenery. We'll be back at our room soon enjoying a cool drink and some fresh pineapple."

"Something has happened. Something very bad. I feel it." And I'd grown to trust my instincts.

"We'll find out soon enough." He pulled back and continued the drive. "Here or at home?"

"I don't know." I sent a quick text to Mags who replied back that everything was fine.

After stopping at a grocery store and paying ridiculous prices for the makings of sandwiches, star fruit, and a pineapple, we arrived at our hut. Minutes later, my sandaled feet propped up on the balcony, we sat on the lanai and enjoyed a late lunch as the fine mist heralded the windsurfers pulling their boards from the water.

Eric handed me the morning newspaper courtesy of the hotel. "You have a reason to be concerned." He tapped the front page.

"Mainland Youth Group Vanished. Chaperones Killed," I read. "Oh, no." I scanned the rest of the article. They suspected the girls had been nabbed by a trafficking ring making the rounds of the islands. "We have to let the police know about Joe Landon and that young man."

"Let's go." We rushed to the car.

Ten minutes later we sat across from an Officer Mack. I suspected his name was short for a Hawaiian volcano or waterfall.

He listened patiently while we told him why we were there. "You're positive?"

"Well, I didn't see them take the girls, only that Landon's supposed daughter seemed frightened—I think she asked for help—and the group of girls following after the young man disappeared." I omitted sharing about the feeling of being followed through the bamboo forest. Without evidence, why make the waters any murkier?

Officer Mack placed a couple of calls before turning back to us. "The young man's name is Albert Manu, and he seems to have disappeared. There's no sign in at any hotel for a Joe Landon. We suspect Manu is the bait used to lure gullible young women and Landon is the leader."

"There would be more in the ring, right?" I asked.

He nodded. "Probably a few on each island. Thank you for the lead, Mr. and Mrs. Drake. We'll take it from here. Enjoy the rest of your honeymoon, and don't go trying to find these men yourselves. They are very dangerous." He chuckled. "Since you've been in the news a few times, you aren't exactly anonymous, ma'am."

"You've heard about me all the way out here?"

He shrugged. "Law enforcement officers have a list."

Great. I'm on a list. "I promise not to get involved." I stood and shook his hand, more than happy to return to the hut with Eric.

We carried blankets to the beach and lay back, watching the palm trees turn dark and magenta and pumpkin color the sky. My heart ached for those girls. In just a few days, at least seven girls had disappeared that we knew of. How many more were being stalked?

For the first time since we arrived, I couldn't wait to get home and leave this particular evil behind us.

Eric reached over and took my hand. "Have faith, sweetheart. We gave Officer Mack a viable lead. Maybe they'll find the girls before they're taken off the island."

"Hopefully." I'd done all that I could. All that was left was prayer for their safe return. "Tomorrow is our last day here."

"Then, real life starts back." He smiled. "It's been a great honeymoon, but I'll be glad to be home."

"Me, too. I miss the dogs and cat." I laughed. Caper often drove me insane with her tendency to get into trouble, but I did love the floppy-eared girl. "I even miss Mags's sarcasm."

"I'm sure your uncle is ready to return the reins of running the community back to you."

"And you miss your mountain."

"Not *my* mountain, but yes, I do. Still, this ocean view is hard to beat." He turned to look at me. "Especially with the woman of my dreams by my side."

Warmth filled me, and some of the peace that fled when I'd read the newspaper article returned. Life was always good with Eric by my side. "What's up for tomorrow?"

"Lahaina. We haven't bought any souvenirs yet."

"I want a muumuu."

"Really?" His brows raised. "Sexy. I'd prefer seeing you in a grass skirt."

"Yep." I laughed. "I'll wear it when I'm old. I also need a new pair of sunglasses."

"I can't wait to see you in the muumuu."

A heavily bearded man walked past us muttering something about pretty girls. I leaped to my feet despite Eric's protests and followed him to the tattered sofa on the beach.

"Excuse me, sir."

He turned and tilted a whiskey bottle to his lips. "You're a pretty girl."

"Thank you. What about the others you mentioned?"

"Girls."

"Do you know where the missing girls are? You said something about pretty girls."

He blinked watery eyes. "In a house."

I bit back irritation at his talking in circles. "This is important. Do you know which house?"

"Pink house."

There had to be dozens of pink houses on the island, right along with blue, green, and yellow. But, it was a start. "Where is this pink house?"

"Here." He waved me away. "I'm going to sleep now. Be careful, pretty girl." He spread out on the sofa and started snoring, the bottle falling to the sand.

I picked it up and propped it next to him. Seems we had another tidbit of information for Officer Mack.

Eric led me back to the hut where I made the call.

"I asked you to stay out of this, Mrs. Drake."

"We were sitting there watching the sunset. I can't help it if we overheard him."

He sighed. "Thank you for this information. We'll be checking all the pink houses on the island."

Two hours later, the phone rang, pulling me from a deep sleep. "Hello?"

"Thanks to you and the homeless man, we rescued four of the girls who were with the youth group," Officer Mack said. "The others are being held somewhere else, according to the girls. Is the homeless man still on the beach?"

"Hold on." I raced outside, Eric on my heels, and sprinted for the sofa.

Yes, the man was still there, but someone had paid him a visit since we'd left him. A knife protruded from his bony chest.

I'd become embroiled in another murder mystery. This time in paradise.

Chapter Four

Lahaina was a quaint fishing village crowded with tourists. Still, I tried to shove the vision of the homeless man from my mind and concentrate on the ocean scene paintings in an art gallery. Today was our last day on Maui and I wanted to soak everything in, doing my best to have more good memories than bad.

After the gallery, where Eric purchased a painting of a sunset over the water and asked for it to be shipped home, we stopped at a local coffee shop for coffee and pastries. While both of us were ready to go home, we weren't in a big hurry for the day to end.

"This has been the best week despite…" I waved my hand.

Eric placed his hand over mine. "I agree. We'll take a lot of trips together, hopefully without the drama of death and kidnapping."

Yes, please. I scanned the tourists strolling past. People laughing, carrying souvenirs, all headed for the farmer's market. I shrugged. There'd be plenty of things left for us to spend our money on.

We finished our mid-morning breakfast and followed the crowd, peeking in shops that sold cheap trinkets but not stopping in any of them. I knew what I wanted and was hoping for something authentic and not mass-produced.

Tables and booths lined the large grassy area. I felt like a kid in a candy store. I purchased a brightly colored tote bag to carry things in, a necklace made of tiny seashells, a vase of beach glass, and a pair of oversized sunglasses.

"I might have to take out a loan when we finish here," Eric said, laughing.

"Oh, pooh." I gave him a playful slap on his arm. "None of it costs close to the painting you bought. Oh, look. There are the muumuus." I rushed to a table where the dresses in every color of the rainbow sat and chose a deep purple one with large pink hibiscus flowers. "I'll model it for you later." I gave my husband an impish grin.

"Only if you also model a grass skirt." He held up a plastic green one.

I shuddered. "That's hideous."

Laughing, he placed the skirt back on the table. "Let's try some sweet rice wrapped in seaweed."

I actually liked the food, despite my reservations about eating seaweed, and happily munched as we weaved through the crowd and the tables. I purchased a monkey made from a coconut for Mags even though I had no idea where she'd put it in her cluttered tiny house. For my uncle, I bought a large conch shell.

"What do you think about a simple meal in our room for our last night?" Eric held up a bunch of grapes. "Fruit, cheese and bread, some champagne?"

"Sounds perfect." I smiled and leaned against him. "No more tourists."

I was glad we'd saved Lahaina for the last day. While the scenic places we'd gone to were crowded, this place was packed, but the market was the perfect ending to our stay. Loaded down with food and souvenirs, we circled the area and arrived back at the car.

Eric stowed our things in the trunk. "Let's get one more snorkeling in before we return the gear."

"The tide pool?"

"I'm thinking more like the big hotel. The water is crystal clear there."

"Okay, but if I hear Jaws, I'm waiting on the beach."

He laughed and slid into the driver's seat. The sun was high overhead when we entered the water at the nearby resort. He was right. The water was so clear I could see the scuba divers at the bottom. The same fish we saw in the tide pool were much larger out in the deep. I smiled. Our tide pool was a nursery in comparison.

Wait a minute. I tapped Eric's shoulder and pointed at a man staring up at us. Joe Landon or whatever his name was. I recognized the glare in his eyes, even through the scuba mask. Next to him, I recognized Alex Manu, his dark hair floating around his shoulders like silk seaweed. Were they having an underwater meeting or prowling for prey? I didn't want to stick around to find out.

We swam to the beach and removed our gear, Eric seeming to be in as big of a hurry to leave as I was. We returned to the shack where we'd rented the snorkeling gear.

"Do you think they'll follow us?" I gripped Eric's hand.

"I don't know, but we need to be super vigilant until we're off this island."

Back in our room, he locked the front door and pulled the curtains on the double doors leading to the patio. My shoulders slumped. "I don't want to be locked in the room. It's our last night to watch the sunset."

He turned from the door and stared at me for a few seconds before nodding. "We watch from the patio so we can move inside fast if we have to."

"You think they'll come for us?"

"I hope not. We don't know anything other than the fact they're still on the island. I need to call Officer Mack." He reached for the room phone and dialed the number to the station while I went to the bedroom to put on my muumuu before gathering the makings for our simple supper and carried it outside.

I glanced around the area. With a clear view of the beach, I could easily see no one was around unless they chose to hide behind one of the palm trees which didn't offer much protection. Two women and two men played shuffleboard to my left. The hut to my right still looked unoccupied. The only thing marring the scene was the crime scene tape fluttering around the tattered sofa. Some of the tension in my shoulders caused by seeing Manu and Landon scuba diving left.

Eric joined me and we ate, watching the ocean kiss the beach. I'd miss this view but looked forward to seeing the sun sparkle on Blue Lake. The tiny community of Heavenly Acres was home and just as beautiful as Hawaii in its own way. I had souvenirs and photos to remind me of this place, along with a few bad memories, too.

"I take it back. You look very sexy in that muumuu." Eric winked and popped a grape in my mouth.

I laughed. "Maybe you should have bought a grass skirt for yourself."

"Not a chance." He glanced at the tropical board shorts he wore. "These are enough for me. I'm not looking forward to the hot uniform I usually wear."

While he looked good, windblown and suntanned, I missed the way he looked in his ranger uniform. Talk about sexy. But, yes, in the humidity where we lived, a lighter weight material would be nice for him.

We resumed eating and watching the sun lower over the water. "If I lived by the ocean, I'd be one of those leathery old women who sits on the beach every day."

"You'd still be beautiful to me."

It still amazed me that Eric could think skinny, petite me was beautiful.

My cell phone rang. "Hey, Mags."

"You received a package. Want me to open it or save it until you return?"

I could tell she was dying to open it. "Go ahead."

"That's weird. Why would someone send you a ring of dead flowers?"

My heart chilled. "Like a lei? You know, the flowers they put around your neck in Hawaii?"

"Yeah. They smell good, but they're shriveled up."

"Does it say who it's from?" My gaze clashed with Eric's.

"Nothing on the outside. There's a card inside that says *From Your Neighbor*. That's it."

Eric's eyes narrowed. "They know where we live. Call Davis."

"Hold onto it for me, Mags. I'm going to have Davis pick it up."

"You're in a mystery without me, aren't you?"

"Don't worry. I have a feeling it'll follow me home." I hung up and dialed Davis's number, putting him on speaker so Eric could hear.

"Yeah?"

I told him about the flowers, which led to filling him in on everything else, then I gave him Officer Mack's number.

"You can't even stay out of trouble on your honeymoon. I feel sorry for Eric."

He'd said that before. "I didn't go looking for this. We were responsible for four girls being found. That's useful. Why would these people want to bring their trouble to Heavenly Acres?"

"Trafficking is becoming a problem here, too. They must think you know more than you do. Be careful. I'll see you when you get back." Click.

He never was much for phone courtesy. "I can't believe this." Tears sprang to my eyes. "Our honeymoon is ruined by what has happened."

"No, sweetheart. It's been perfect." Eric's lips

twitched. "You add excitement everywhere you go, and I wouldn't have it any other way. Don't worry. We'll get through this just as we always have."

Eric double-checked the door locks before we went to bed. I tossed and turned, wrestling with the sheets for hours, glad I could sleep on the plane.

When the alarm went off in the morning, I groaned and threw aside the covers. "Let's go home."

I constantly glanced over my shoulder at the car rental counter and then on our way to the terminal to board our plane for the main island. Once there, I studied the face of every person we passed on the way to our gate, knowing Manu and Landon wouldn't be brazen enough to openly follow us at the airport. They'd never make it through security. Still, I couldn't shake the feeling of being watched.

We had an eight-hour layover in Los Angeles. Fatigue weighed me down. We tried stretching out on a booth in a closed restaurant, but security ran us off. We sat in hard chairs at our gate and slept with our heads leaning against each other. Not ideal, but it was the best we could do.

I opened my eyes a couple of hours later to see the seats around us filling up. One man stared at us from a couple of rows away. Surely we weren't the first people to fall asleep in the airport. In no mood for rude people, I glared back until he dropped his gaze.

I rummaged in the tote bag I'd bought on Maui and pulled out a water bottle we'd purchased from one of the stores in the airport. Now that we were on our journey home, I couldn't wait for the trip to end. Eight hours was far too long to wait in an airport.

The man two rows over stared again. "Can I help you?" I called out loud enough to wake Eric.

"You look familiar," the man said with a shrug.

"Well, I'm not anyone famous." I took a big drink of the water and handed the bottle to Eric.

"My apologies."

"What's going on?" Eric whispered.

"I've caught that man staring quite a few times."

"Boredom."

"Maybe." Still my spider senses were tingling overtime. "I need to use the restroom."

"I'm coming with you. I'll wait outside the door, but you aren't going anywhere alone." Eric stood and helped me to my feet.

After taking care of business, I stared in the mirror at eyes red from lack of sleep and washed my hands, using the water to tame my hair so I looked less like Medusa and more like myself. Had Davis found out where the lei came from? Had Officer Mack rescued any more girls? Despite my resolve not to get involved, I had a heavy feeling the decision would be made for me.

Was I in any danger of being taken? At the age of twenty-seven, my size made me look a lot younger. The homeless man had called me a pretty girl, same as the abducted teenagers. Was he warning me?

I shuddered, shaking off the feeling of doom, and left the restroom to join Eric, again feeling as if we were being watched.

Chapter Five

After picking up our car from the airport extended-stay lot, Eric drove us to my house where we collapsed in bed, fully clothed. A pounding on the door woke us. I peeked at the time. We'd gotten four hours of sleep. Not nearly enough. I groaned and tossed off the covers.

"I'll get it." Eric pulled a pistol from the shelf above his head.

"When did you start sleeping with the gun close at hand?" I hated guns.

"When things got serious between you and me, not to mention my own near-death experiences. Knowing how you feel about guns, I didn't tell you I had one stashed in your house for easy access." He gave me a quick kiss and headed down the stairs to answer the door.

My tiny house filled with people and pets as Davis entered first, followed by Mags, Larry, the dogs, and my cat, Sherlock. The cat immediately jumped on the windowsill and turned his back, expressing his displeasure at me having left him for so long. Caper ran straight into my arms, licking my face, while Hershey did the same to Eric.

"The lei has been taken in as evidence," Davis said, getting right down to business. "No information as to where it came from."

I knew it had come from Landon which I'd continue to call him until we learned his real name. "I don't want it anyway."

"This is serious, CJ. These trafficking rings are everywhere. They won't have any qualms about stopping anyone who gets in their way. I've said this at least a hundred times, but don't get involved."

"I don't plan on it." I set Caper down. "I didn't mean to on Maui. If I hadn't heard the homeless man muttering to himself, I would have gone along my ignorant way, none the wiser." Not true at all. I'd had trouble sleeping, worrying about the group of girls.

He pierced me with a sharp gaze. "Don't go anywhere alone. Do I need to have Ann protect you?"

"No, I have Eric." Ann Lowery, once a police officer now a private investigator, had been my bodyguard on more than one occasion. While she was now my close friend, I didn't want her staying with me and my new husband.

"Your husband has a job. He can't be with you all the time." He shook his head. "I strongly urge you to contact Ann."

"I'll think about it." I saw my friend on a regular basis since she rented my grandmother's house from me. I hadn't been able to move back after Grams's death and now couldn't believe I'd live anywhere but Heavenly Acres.

After Davis left, I handed out the gifts we'd purchased and made coffee. As it dripped into the first cup, I stared out the small window over my single sink. It looked as if my handyman, Roy Olson, had kept the place up well in my absence.

"Every house is full," Larry said. "I rented the last one, number twenty-two yesterday." He patted my shoulder. "I'm glad you're back. Some of these people are needy."

I laughed. "They aren't that bad."

"Well, I expect you'll make the rounds introducing yourself as the manager. The campground is just starting to receive guests now that the weather is turning nice." He took the first cup and sat on the sofa.

"Any strangers lurking around?" Eric asked.

"Not that we've noticed." Larry sighed. "Of course, the bad guys could be living right under our noses, and we wouldn't know. Thanks for the shell. I'll use it to scare Mags on occasion."

True. It had happened before. What better way to keep an eye on things than to rent one of the houses?

"If you blow that shell when I'm not expecting it," Mags said, "I'll break up with you."

"We can't have that now, can we?" He chuckled and kissed her cheek.

I couldn't help but wonder if my uncle would ever marry my friend. I hoped so. If anyone could keep Mags in check, it was Larry.

Eric stepped up behind me and wrapped his arms around my waist. "I don't go back to work until tomorrow. Want me to make the rounds with you?"

I turned, smiling up at him. "Every day, if it's

possible."

"Okay, you lovebirds," Mags called from the sofa. "We need to discuss how to keep this ring out of our community. I say we resume the neighborhood watch."

I turned reluctantly from Eric and handed him the next cup of coffee. "The watch has worked before, but no one patrols alone."

"Danny went with me before," she said. "I'm sure he will again. You can take Eric."

"I'll patrol with you." Larry frowned. "How can a seventeen-year-old keep you safer than I can?"

"But you're so busy."

"I'm rich and retired. I can do whatever I want whenever I want."

"Okay. Then you go with me. I'll head out and have other people sign up so everyone only has to do one night a week. Less if more people agree to help." Looking quite satisfied with herself, Mags declined the coffee I offered her. "Already had two."

Sweet. That meant I got mine quicker. I sat on the sofa and propped my feet on the coffee table. With my brain still fuzzy from lack of sleep and jet lag, I let the others talk around me. Let them come up with a plan and then tell me what they wanted me to do.

I smiled as Danny and sixteen-year-old, Rose Flower, strolled past the window, hand in hand. It appeared they'd moved past the point of friendship. It was bound to happen sooner or later with as much time as they spent together.

"Lucy put another floor on her house," Mags said. "Looks atrocious."

"Really?" With five growing children, I was

actually surprised that Rose's mother hadn't built on sooner or moved to a regular house. "Did the city approve?"

"I reckon. She hired a contractor. Whoever heard of a three-story tiny house? It looks like a chimney rising straight into the sky."

Mags had an opinion about everything. I'd make up my own mind, and since my uncle had no objections as the owner of the land the Flower house sat on, I couldn't say much. The house wouldn't block my view of the mountain or the lake, so all was good.

"Looks like we have Mondays," Eric said, pulling my attention back to the others.

"Any night is fine." At least it wasn't winter. The winter nights were frigid this close to the mountain.

Larry and Mags left, leaving me and Eric to take a drive around the community and campground. I printed off the reservation sheet, then followed my husband to the gator where the two dogs already sat in the tail bed.

We started across the lake, passing the chapel where we were married. I was glad to see that no one had vandalized it. Feeling that a church should be left open for folks to pray as needed, I left it unlocked.

A group of young men camped in number five. I eyed them with suspicion as we drove by. Were they predators? Would I ever look at handsome men without thinking they were up to no good? It wasn't fair, but after the way Manu lured the youth group, I wasn't taking any chances.

"Should we enact a curfew in the community to keep the young girls inside after ten o'clock?"

"It wouldn't hurt," Eric said. "But it might cause a panic. How many teen girls are there?"

"Roy's daughter just turned fourteen, and Rose is sixteen, not to mention her sister Daisy is twelve now. Is that too young to be of interest?"

"No. Maybe just alert Roy and Lucy of the possible danger for now. Of course, Mags will create the panic we want to avoid when she goes around getting volunteers to take a night of patrol."

I nodded. He was right. Without knowing whether Landon's crew was even in the state, why cause undue worry? "I don't know if any of the new renters have daughters, but we'll find out soon enough." Just as I did in the past, I'd do everything in my power to keep my community safe. That didn't necessarily mean I was getting involved in anything, right?

There were no campers camping that hadn't paid their fee, and more would arrive the next day. I glanced at the paper in my hand, then folded it and stuck it in my pocket. I didn't need it in order to know which houses were no longer empty. Only six had been vacant when Eric and I left on our honeymoon, and now they were full. Twenty through twenty-five. The last of the houses in the circle.

Eric parked in front of number twenty and waited in the cart while I approached the front door. I knocked and a gray-haired lady answered the door. "Yes?"

"I'm CJ Tur...Drake, the manager here and wanted to introduce myself. Is there anything you need, Mrs. Wentworth?"

She pursed her lips together. "I have a leak under

the kitchen sink. Your handyman is coming sometime today to fix it. Other than that, all is good. Thank you." She moved to close the door.

"Please don't hesitate to let me know." I glanced down to see three cats peering at me from around her ankles. "Cutie-pies."

"The lease didn't say I couldn't have pcts."

"Pets are very welcome here." My eyes widened as another cat appeared. "How many do you have?"

She squared her shoulders. "Ten. After my husband died, I surrounded myself with these companions."

Mercy. That's a lot in such a tiny space. I kept my smile in place and rejoined Eric. "She isn't very friendly, but I doubt she's anyone to worry about."

He narrowed his eyes. "You're going door to door to see if anyone is up to no good, aren't you?"

"In addition to introducing myself. I need to be aware of what goes on here."

"I just felt a gray hair grow on my head."

"Poor baby." I patted his leg as he drove to the next house. No one was home, but I knew from the records Larry left that a Mr. and Mrs. Smith lived there. No children. Number twenty-two's occupants were also not home, which led me to believe the occupants had day jobs. I'd come back later.

A young couple, the Fosters, expecting a baby soon, lived in number twenty-three. I went through the same spiel as I'd done with Mrs. Wentworth.

"We love it here," Fae Foster said. "This little place is inexpensive enough for us to save up until we need a bigger place." She rubbed her stomach. "It's perfect for us and a baby."

"I'm glad you've settled in." Maybe the community could throw her a baby shower.

A single mom with a teenage daughter lived in twenty-four. I started to warn Mrs. Washington that her daughter, Dayshenay, could be a target but didn't. Not until we had a reason.

A single man lived in twenty-five. From his tousled hair, I reckoned I woke him. After making my apologies and him telling me he didn't need anything, I rejoined Eric.

"Any suspects?" He raised his brows.

"Not really. I'll have to come back later to meet those who weren't home, but I've learned from the past that looks can be deceiving. For all I know, Mrs. Wentworth could be the leader of the trafficking ring."

He laughed. "Yeah, she looks the type. Can't trust those cat lovers."

I joined in his laughter, knowing I'd keep a sharp eye on all my tenants, just in case.

Eric gave my hand a gentle squeeze. "Don't get involved."

"I'm not."

"Uh huh."

"I'm not." I tilted my head. "Unless a reason presents itself, I'm staying out of this one. I'll be too busy working and being your wife."

He laughed harder at that statement and turned us toward home.

Chapter Six

Life settled into a routine with Eric heading to work each morning and me making the rounds. That morning though, it being Eric's day off, I sat in a deck chair next to the lake, sipped my coffee, and watched as a large flatbed truck delivered Eric's house. Today was the first step in making our two houses one. Caper and Hershey, both on leashes, watched from next to my chair, ears on alert for an opportunity to bark.

While I supervised from a safe distance away, Eric helped a forklift move his house next to mine. He tossed me a grin as the house settled into place with a thud. A massive forklift then lifted the house and moved it as close as possible to mine. The precision amazed me.

Eric had told me the next step would be to put new siding on the two houses to make them look like one before he tore down the separating outer walls. We'd be living in a construction zone for a while.

Davis's car pulled to a stop. After exiting his car,

he marched my way, a stack of fliers in his hand. The grave expression on his face told me he wasn't here for a pleasant visit. "We've had a girl disappear in town. I want you to hand these out to your tenants and post one on the board at the campground." He handed me the sheets. "She's known for running away, so this doesn't mean the traffickers are in our midst, but we're playing things safe."

My blood chilled. I glanced down to see that a ten o'clock curfew had been placed and a warning for parents to be vigilant in knowing where their children were. "You specify children. You think the boys are targeted, too?"

"Most of the time it's girls," he said, "but boys have disappeared, too. It's better to be safe than sorry."

I nodded and got to my feet. "I'll distribute these right now." Leaving the dogs where they were, out of harm's way, I hurried to my golf cart and set off for the campgrounds. I couldn't believe that evil might have once again arrived in our sleepy little town. Maybe I should move for the safety of the town's residents. Nothing seemed to happen until I arrived at Heavenly Acres.

Not true. My first day there I'd arrived amidst a rash of burglaries. I felt a little better. It had to be the revolving door of tenants that caused the problems. Maybe we needed to do a more thorough background check before letting them sign a lease.

I tacked one of the fliers on the community board at the campground and frowned as a family with three young girls glanced over.

"What's that?" The father asked, reading over my

shoulder. "We were told this was a safe place to camp with our family."

I forced a smile. "It is. We're just cautioning parents to err on the side of caution."

He didn't look convinced as he rushed his family back to their camper. I winced as the door slammed, hoping he didn't intend to keep his girls locked up for the remainder of their stay. What kind of a spring break would that be?

After making the rounds of the campground, a duty I shared with Eric, I headed back to the tiny houses to start the unpleasant task of dropping off fliers at each house. When I'd started working as manager, there had only been twenty houses. Uncle Larry had expanded to twenty-five since last summer. We had no more room to expand, thankfully.

Dave Lincoln, the on-again-off-again boyfriend of Lucy Flower glanced at the flier I handed him, then toward the towering number six. "I'll be staying with Lucy and her kids for a while."

"That's a great idea." The more eyes watching over the children, the better.

Number four, once the home of Amber—Mags's granddaughter until she married Davis—had recently been purchased by a Loren Weston. The handsome man in his mid-forties smiled as he opened the door.

"I'd heard the new manager was a looker," he said.

I smiled and handed him a flier. "We've met before I left on my honeymoon, Mr. Weston."

"Sure, but a little flattery never hurts, and a week without seeing your pretty face is a week too long.

Your husband is a lucky man."

I laughed at his not-so-subtle flirtation. "Take care."

"You, too. You might not be a teen, but you're lovely enough for anyone to snatch."

I shook off his foreboding words and headed for number five. Mags would be upset if she didn't get a flier since she insisted on being kept apprised of everything that went on in the community.

"Let me get my keys," she said. "I'm coming with you. You aren't supposed to be wandering off alone. Besides, I can't concentrate on my soaps with all that racket coming from your place."

I rolled my eyes and waited while she locked her doors. "I'm only handing these out, not wandering off."

"Still, Davis issued an order not to be alone. You arrived on my doorstep alone."

Sighing, I led the way to number six. "Hello, Sage," I greeted the six-year-old. "Is your mother home?"

"Mom!" His yell pierced my eardrum.

"Hey, CJ, Mags." A tired Lucy stepped up behind her son.

"We're handing these out." I watched her face pale as she read.

"Should I be worried?" A frown creased her brow.

"Cautious, especially with Rose and Daisy. One missing girl doesn't necessarily mean anything more than a possible runaway, but you can't be too careful." I told her of Dave's intention to stay with her in the meantime.

She gave a nervous laugh. "Good thing I've expanded. With these children growing, room is in short supply. I'd move, but this house is paid for."

"Same reason I stay," Mags said. "Plus, we look after each other here."

We continued making the rounds and left number thirteen, a larger house where Roy Olson, the handyman, lived with his family. He took one look at the flier, then at the playground where Amanda and Dayshenay sat on swings, lazily pushing forward and back. "Danny! Go get Amanda and tell her to come home."

"Why?" His son frowned, barely looking up from the cell phone in his hand.

"Because I said so."

"Does that mean I have to keep an eye on Teddy? Isn't eleven old enough to play by himself?" He pushed grumpily to his feet. "I was texting Rose."

"Do that later." Roy turned his attention back to me. "This is going to give Tammy an anxiety attack."

"I'm sorry," I said. "Just following Davis's orders."

He nodded. "Does your hubby need any help on that combination of houses?"

"Maybe." I grinned. "Eric will appreciate any help. He's only off today and wants to at least get the two combined with new siding."

Roy yelled through the door to let his wife know where he was going, then climbed into his golf cart and sped away. We truly did have good neighbors for the most part.

"That went well, I think," Mags said. "No panicking or running around screaming into the night.”

"It isn't night yet." I glanced around the area, smiling at the unhappy Amanda led home by her brother. "As long as everyone remains vigilant, we'll all be fine."

"I'll keep my eyes out for handsome young men." Mags wiggled her eyebrows. "It's a sacrifice I'm willing to make."

I laughed, imagining my almost sixty-year-old friend surrounded by teenagers and young adults. She'd be in her element, but I'd feel sorry for them if the teens acted inappropriately. My friend had a very sharp tongue. It was like a sport seeing her riled up.

Since she insisted on coming home with me to make sure the men didn't make my house as ugly as she insisted the Flower home now was, I left her at the picnic table and went inside to make sandwiches in the middle of a construction zone.

The hammering of siding on the new front and back of the house, which would now sport two small porches, caused a similar pounding in my head. I made ham and swiss sandwiches to go around, added a bag of chips, made a pitcher of lemonade, and joined Mags at the table.

Since all the houses sported white siding with different colored window trim, my house now had green windows on one half and blue on the other. That was going to bother me. "How do you feel about painting?"

"Hate it." Mags grabbed a sandwich.

I shrugged and figured I'd have to paint the trim myself, then. Unless… "Roy, can Danny handle a paintbrush?"

"Sure, he can."

"Would he paint all my window trims either blue or green? I don't care which, use whatever paint you have, but I really need them to be the same color."

Eric laughed. "My wife has a bit of OCD."

"Don't you want it to look like one house and not two stuck together?" I raised my brows.

"It will. I'll have the walls inside taken down before we go to bed tonight, thanks to Roy's help."

Good. I relaxed a bit. "Take a break and come eat."

The men stopped their work and joined us. Roy asked about our honeymoon, I filled him in on Manu luring the girls.

"So, as long as our daughters aren't around any good-looking boys, they're safe?"

"I'd take away their cell phones," Eric said, "but that's just me, although Davis did have phones and computers mentioned as a hazard on the flier. A lot of girls are lured by an adult pretending to be their age, asking them to meet up somewhere." He glanced around. "With the park, the campgrounds, the lake, the cathedral, the mountain…there's no end to places people could meet and not be seen easily."

I followed his gaze. He was right. With all the trees, foliage, and buildings, there were a lot of places for a predator to hide. "How would Hershey feel about sleeping on the front porch for a few nights? She'd be a good warning system if someone is out wandering around."

"That's actually a good idea." Eric smiled.

"What about the neighborhood watch?" Mags tilted her head. "She'll bark as soon as someone starts patrolling."

"Which a quick look outside will confirm," I said. "I know we have security cameras around, but a dog is still a very good warning system."

"It can't hurt." Eric took a sip of lemonade. "Perfect."

While Roy finished the siding and Danny started on the window trim with blue paint, Eric headed inside to start cutting into the walls. Poor Sherlock. When I carried the lunch dishes inside, he peered at me from the loft, clearly unpleased with the day's events.

"Think of how much room you'll have," I told him. "Lots of windows to watch out of. It'll be over soon." Thankfully. Once the walls were down, Eric would put something over the gap in the floor where the two floors stopped so we wouldn't fall through.

I kept telling myself how much better it would be when finished and went outside to rejoin Mags who scribbled on a piece of paper. I peered over her shoulder. "What are you doing?"

"Writing down suspects in the community and the possible targets."

"Why is Dave Lincoln's name on there?"

"Because he's a single male now living right under the same roof with Rose and Daisy. We can't trust anyone."

Dave has lived there longer than I had. If we did have a predator in our midst, it wouldn't be him. Tonight was my and Eric's night to patrol. I prayed it would be a peaceful one.

Chapter Seven

At ten o'clock, Eric carried the last pieces of the wall to a heap of debris in the yard and clipped a leash on Hershey's collar. "I'll be ready to hit the pillow as soon as we're finished with our patrol. Construction is hard work."

"It looks great, though." I attached a leash to Caper's collar. Once upon a time, I'd let her roam ahead but after multiple times of her digging up diamonds, I kept her close at hand. "I can see the final picture."

"I can't wait to get started combining the kitchens." He leaned forward and kissed me. "It feels like a mansion compared to before."

I laughed and stepped outside to wait as he locked the front door. There was a time when I didn't need to lock my door every time I wandered the community, but I'd had enough of almost being killed. "Are we taking the golf cart?" I asked when Eric headed to our left.

"I thought we'd walk the community, then take

the golf cart past the cathedral before walking the campgrounds. It'll be harder for someone to see us coming if we're on foot."

"You think we'll actually see something?" I swallowed past the lump rising in my throat.

"Not really. I guess those crime shows you watch are rubbing off on me. But, I'm not taking any chances." His teeth flashed in the moonlight as he handed me a flashlight. "Ready?"

I nodded, pretending not to see the gun holster on his belt. It would be at least midnight by the time we patrolled both places and were able to head to bed. I wasn't thirty yet and already thought like an old lady when it came to sleep.

Lights were still on in most of the houses, but some flickered out as we passed. The squeak of a swing drew our attention to the playground. Neither Caper or Hershey seemed alarmed, but we crept ahead and ducked behind a bush.

Eric groaned and stood, shining his flashlight on Danny and Rose leaning forward to share a kiss. "Curfew was at ten, you two. Don't you know how dangerous it is out here?"

"She's with me," Danny said, straightening. "I patrolled with Mags before, and I can protect Rose."

"This isn't before. Teenage boys disappear, too." Eric's severe tone left no room for argument. "Being out here puts Rose at risk. If you care about her, you'll take her home right now and not take her out after dark again."

"Yes, sir." Danny grabbed Rose's hand and made a dash for her house.

"Teenagers." Eric shook his head. "That boy

wouldn't be able to live with himself if his actions, or hers, caused something to happen to her."

The door opened in number four, and two young men stepped out. One dark, one light, they laughed and strolled in the opposite direction.

Why would Loren be having young people visit after curfew? I made a move forward, only to be stopped by Eric. "They look older than sixteen. The curfew only applies to sixteen and under."

"Shouldn't we question them anyway?" I frowned. "I've never seen them before, and Loren doesn't have a son."

"If we see them again during our rounds, we'll ask some questions."

As we passed Loren's house, his light turned off. Instinct told me something wasn't right about the two boys visiting him so late, but since it was spring break, I shoved aside the feeling of unease. I'd learned that if something was wrong, it would show itself soon enough. Unfortunately, often at my attempted demise.

A complete circle of the community showed no one else outside, so Eric and I drove the golf cart past the cathedral, slowing to look inside, then parked at the back entrance to the campground.

Fires burned in several pits, people drank and laughed around the fires, but no one wandered outside of their own site. "Looks like they're following the curfew," I said. Not that it was unusual. There was also a noise curfew starting at ten p.m.

We waved at the group of young men still camping during what I'd learned was their spring break from college. They raised red cups in a salute our way. As we passed, I glanced back to see one of them step into the woods behind their site.

"Why can't he use the restroom provided? It isn't that far away." We worked hard to keep the bathrooms and showers clean.

"He's a young man drinking beer. The woods are easier." Eric chuckled. "It's one of the benefits to being male."

"Ha." I gripped his arm. "Wait. There's the two young men from Loren's house." I ducked behind a trash bin.

"Way to look conspicuous." Eric hauled me to my feet. "Although it does seem strange to see them at Loren's and now here."

The two came from a large camper. When they exited, two more men went in. I frowned, counting those milling about. "You're only allowed ten people per site. There's fifteen, not counting who is inside."

"Definitely a violation." He handed me Hershey's leash before pulling his ID from his pocket. "Wait here."

No way. I moved close enough to hear what was said.

"Who is responsible for this campsite?" Eric asked handing up his badge. "I'm Ranger Drake and there are more people here than are allowed per camp rules."

All laughter and conversation ceased as everyone turned to stare at him. I stepped into the light, holding up my cell phone to start recording in case of trouble. I pressed the record button.

Someone knocked on the door to the camper, and a man who looked to be in his middle forties stepped out. "I'm Bill Harris. I rented this site."

Eric repeated what he'd said about there being too many people.

"My apologies. I'm having a birthday party, and well, the guest list got a little out of hand." The man grinned.

"No women?"

He motioned his head toward the camper. "Only a couple, but they're ready to go to bed. Lightweights, you know? You're welcome to come look inside. Isn't it a bit late for you to be out?"

"No, sir. We have a Neighborhood Watch around here."

Please don't go inside. I had a bad feeling in the pit of my stomach.

Eric glanced over the man's shoulder but didn't ask to go inside. *Thank you, God.* I felt that if he entered, he'd never come out.

Harris promised to break up the group, and I slipped my cell phone into my pocket. I planned on letting Davis know as soon as we were out of sight of these men, so he could decide whether it warranted investigating or not. See? I was not interfering. I was leaving whatever this was to the authorities.

Eric joined me and took my arm, hurrying me along. "Something isn't right. We need to contact Davis."

"I recorded the whole thing. I'll send him a text and attach the video."

Three minutes later, Davis ordered us home at once and said he was on his way with backup. I was more than happy to get back to the golf cart and head for home.

Knowing I wouldn't be able to sleep until hearing from Davis, I sat on the front porch with Eric, lights off, dogs at our feet, and stared toward the campground. Flashing red and blue lights lit up the night sky. The cavalry had arrived. Would things be found innocent or criminal?

"Wouldn't you think women would be outside partying the same as the men?" Eric asked. "I know it was a large camper, but to go to sleep during a party at only eleven o'clock doesn't ring true to me."

"Me either. That's why I recorded it. I wanted proof if you were harmed."

"My little guardian angel." He chuckled. "What if they had attacked? I would've wanted you to run."

"And leave you behind?" I widened my eyes. "I couldn't do that."

"Then you would have been captured. I know how old you are, but sometimes when I look at you, I think I've robbed the cradle."

"You're sweet. Kiss me." I leaned toward him. I'd never tire of the feel of his lips on mine.

Shouts carried across the lake's surface pulling my attention back to the campground. A gunshot rang out, then another. So things hadn't been innocent after all. Dread filled my veins with ice.

"Come on. We might as well go to bed," Eric said, climbing to his feet. "We won't know anything for hours and its best to stay out of Davis's way." He held out his hand. "I'll leave Hershey on the porch."

"Will she be all right?"

He nodded. "She's trained not to eat anything unless I give it to her."

So his mind had drifted in the same direction as

mine. He'd thought of the possibility of poison, too. After my initial request of leaving the dog outside, my mind had run a gamut of unpleasant possibilities.

A knock on the door and Caper's frenzied barking, not to mention Hershey's from outside, had Eric and me bolting from the bed. I glanced at the clock. Nine a.m.

"They're knocking on the porch of the other half of the house." I tossed aside the sheet. "Guess whoever it is doesn't want to get too close to your dog."

"My sweet girl can be ferocious when she needs to be." Eric motioned for me to wait while he went to answer the door. "Hey, Davis."

"Good idea tying your dog out front," he said, entering the house. "I need to talk to the two of you."

"Do you want coffee?" I headed for the kitchen.

"Yes, please. It's been a long night." He sat in one of the chairs. We now had several since combining the houses.

He waited to continue until we all had coffee in our hands and were seated. "The camper contained our missing teen girl from town, plus two others. I won't go into the sordid details of why she was there or why the men were. We've rescued her, two men are dead, and I think the two of you might be in grave danger. You were seen filming Eric's conversation with the cell phone, then we showed up. Doesn't take a genius to figure out who told us. We stopped by number four. The man had already vacated the property."

I clutched Eric's hand, tears burning my eyes from what that young girl had endured. "What now?"

"Be vigilant. Don't go anywhere alone. Not even you, Eric. I'm sorry, but I'm strongly suggesting that you hire Ann to accompany you in your park ranger duties. If CJ stays close to home with Mags or Larry at her side, she ought to be safe enough." He smirked. "Who am I kidding? Mags is as bad as CJ at getting into trouble. I'll have Milton accompany Eric, and Ann can stay here. You have two bedrooms now."

"So much for honeymoon bliss with a third wheel around." I scowled.

"If you're dead, the honeymoon would definitely be over." He stood. "Thanks for the coffee. This is what happens when trouble follows you home."

"But why here? Why not a big city?"

He shrugged. "Hopefully we'll find out before anyone else is harmed." He pulled a sheet of paper in a plastic bag from his pocket. "Found this on your car, under the windshield wiper. It explains a lot."

I read, "You helped the cops find them, now we'll need more to meet our quota." I glanced up to meet Eric's worried gaze. They, whoever they were, were here.

Chapter Eight

Mags waltzed in wearing a long, curly blonde wig, lots of makeup, and leggings with a cropped top that barely covered her middle. I spewed coffee out my nose while the two men simply stared with wide eyes.

"What kind of a getup is that?" Davis's voice rose shrill.

"I'm willing to be bait." She posed. "I've got my Taser in my bra, and I know how to use it."

"God help us all. Don't be ridiculous. Go home and change. You're insane."

The laughter I couldn't contain burst forth so hard I clutched my stomach. "This is outlandish, even for you, my friend."

"Why? Because I'm too old?" She narrowed her eyes. "No one can tell until they get close."

"I'm not saying it again." Davis's voice changed to hoarse. "If you make one move toward interfering in my investigation, I'll arrest you."

She yanked off the wig. "You…well, I can't say

what I'm thinking right now." She stormed out of the house muttering that he wouldn't have caught killers in the past if not for her investigative skills.

Davis shook his head. "At least my wife isn't as crazy as her grandmother. I called Ann as soon as I found the note on your car. She'll be here soon."

"I'm already here." Ann entered, suitcase in hand. "Who burnt Mags's rear end? She glared and passed me without saying hello.

"I did." Davis exhaled heavily. "Sorry, CJ, Eric, but things are heating up fast. I'm closing down the campgrounds until further notice. Be careful. Don't go to work until Milton arrives. Then, the two of you can make sure the campers are following my orders to vacate."

"Why close the campground?" I asked.

"Because watching over these twenty-five houses will be enough to keep the department busy."

After he left, Ann glanced around. "Wow. So much room. I'm assuming I'm to sleep in Eric's loft?"

I nodded. "It's good to see you but not under these circumstances." Privacy was now a thing of the past, at least for now.

While she moved her things to the other loft, Eric took my hand and led me outside. He cupped my face. "Be careful, CJ. I know how vigilant Ann is, but I'll still worry."

"You do the same." I leaned into him. Officer Milton would watch Eric's back, but the trafficking ring seemed larger than I'd originally thought. What if my husband and Milton were outnumbered in the woods?

Milton arrived in an unmarked car. He stepped out of his vehicle wearing khaki shorts, dark green knee socks, and a shirt that strained across his stomach. "Do I look the part?"

"What's up with the costumes today?" Eric asked. "First Mags, now you."

Milton patted his paunch of a belly. "Should I change? I thought I'd be less conspicuous if I wasn't wearing my police uniform."

"You're fine." Eric cast me an amused look and leaned close to whisper, "At least your guard looks normal."

I giggled and kissed him. "He'll keep you amused all day. Hope he doesn't pop a button. It might put out an eye."

Eric and Milton left in the gator shortly after. I cast a glance toward the vacant number four, expecting to see crime scene tape fluttering from the porch railing. I guess seeing the two young men there and at the campground wasn't enough reason to secure the property. My first order of business for the day would be to get the house ready for a new tenant.

I turned as Ann stepped outside. "Does Davis consider Loren Weston a suspect?"

"Yes." She glanced toward the house. "There was tape on that house when I arrived."

Disappointment slammed into me. So much for it not being a crime scene. "Do you think Davis removed it?"

She shrugged. "Easy enough to find out." She sent a text and received a quick reply. "No, he didn't remove it and told us to stay away."

"I planned on cleaning the place." I should have

kept my mouth shut. If I had, I could be snooping right now. "There might be a clue in there."

"What if I found you in there, and that's why I texted Davis?" She grinned and arched a brow. "You wouldn't have known the tape had been removed, although he'll be angry that you went off alone."

The police officer Ann would have forbidden me to go inside. The private investigator/bodyguard Ann wasn't as prone to do things by the book. I actually suspected she enjoyed breaking the rules.

"I'll make it quick." If I did find something, I'd have to either lie to Davis or take the consequences of telling the truth. I'd take the lecture. It wouldn't be the first time.

We rushed to number four. I reached out and pushed the door open. Footsteps sounded behind us. I whirled to see Mags looking normal.

"Investigating without me?"

"Nope. Wouldn't dream of it. You can come in with me. Ann will keep watch."

"Just like the old days before you got married." She squeezed past me.

"I've been married a little over two weeks, Mags, and we aren't getting involved. I'm simply seeing what amount of work I need to do to rent the place." I entered the house and glanced around.

"Right."

Loren had left in a hurry. A laptop charger minus the laptop sat on the kitchen counter. Papers littered the floor. Three glasses sat in the sink.

"What are we looking for?" Mags asked, heading for the bedroom.

"Anything pertaining to sex trafficking or other

crimes." I hoped we wouldn't find anything, but Loren's quick departure didn't look good.

"Here." Mags handed me rubber gloves.

"You're getting too good at this."

"Someone has to keep a level head."

I snorted at the thought of Mags being the level-headed one. Especially after her getup earlier. "I don't think you qualify on the best of days."

"Hush and get to work."

I opened cabinets and looked under furniture. Not finding anything, I moved to the refrigerator. Neatly stacked plastic containers, a half-gallon jug of milk, and two slices of leftover pizza. Yep, it looked like a bachelor's fridge. Except…I bent and studied one of the containers. The contents didn't look like food.

I removed the container and opened the lid. Several four-by-six photographs stared up at me. I spread them on the counter. My heart dropped to my toes to see every teenage girl in Heavenly Acres photographed. Why hadn't Loren taken these with him? I returned the photos to the container and joined Ann outside.

"Call Davis. I have all the evidence we need against Loren."

She frowned and made the call before turning back to me. "Why leave them behind?"

My mouth dropped open. "What if he didn't take the photos? What if someone is framing him?"

"Then why run?"

"That's the question to be answered, isn't it?" Mags handed Ann a towel covered with blood. "Maybe he didn't leave on his own."

We returned to my house to wait for Davis. He arrived within minutes. "I was nearby." He joined the three of us women at the picnic table. "I should be angry that you entered a crime scene, but no one else thought to look in the fridge." He glanced at the photos and the towel. "I'll put out a missing person on Weston, but I'm not holding onto a lot of hope for his safe return. CJ, I need you to see a sketch artist about the two young men you saw leaving Weston's house."

"They're in the video I sent you." I pulled it up on my phone and pointed them out. "Weren't they there when you arrived?"

"No." I didn't think his expression could grow any graver. "Those two may be the lures. Let me know right away if you see them again. I'll pay a visit to each of the parents of the girls in those photos and warn them. I don't like this at all."

Neither did I. The local police department didn't have the manpower to handle this on their own. "Are you calling in the FBI?"

"I don't have a choice. I can't keep you from doing your job, CJ., and I also know you'll ask questions while doing it, but I don't want you to leave Heavenly Acres. Not even with Ann. You already know too much, which puts you at a huge risk."

"Not to mention I've already received a warning note."

"Maybe you should reconsider using me as bait." Mags crossed her arms.

"Absolutely not." He rolled his eyes. "If we use anyone, it will be an undercover police officer. You stay out of this. If anything happens to you, Amber will have my head. I'm here way too much for this to be good for my health." Weariness wrinkled his face as he left us.

"Now what?" Mags asked.

"Nothing except help watch over the girls of this community." I let Caper out of the house and tied her to her lead line. Caper wasn't much protection, but she would bark if someone tried sneaking up on us.

"How do you plan on doing that?" Ann asked.

"I'm thinking."

"Don't hurt yourself," Mags said, grinning.

"The only thing I can think of is to keep driving around the property. The kids return to school tomorrow. I can sit at the bus stop when they leave and when they arrive." I watched as Davis approached the Flower family's house.

Poor Lucy had enough responsibility being the single mother of five children. She relied on Rose a lot to help with the younger ones. How would she manage work and keep her daughters safe at the same time?

"Ann is needed more at that house than here," I said.

"I'll be out there every evening until I know each girl is safely home. Once Eric is with you, I'll make the rounds. You'll be safe locked in your house for an hour."

Knowing she planned to be an extra set of eyes in addition to whoever was on watch each night eased some of my worry. "Who's on watch tonight?"

"Me and Larry," Mags said. "The neighborhood will be safe under our sharp eyes."

"I don't think the girls will be taken during the night. Somehow, they'll be lured away in broad daylight, just like the girls in Hawaii. We can't predict how or when. That's what's so scary. Look at the poor girl from town."

Ann nodded. "She did run away from home after an argument with her mother about a boy she'd met online. Now, she'll struggle with the aftermath for a very long time. We can't let that happen to the girls here."

"I can't imagine any of them running away. If something happens, it'll be during their normal activities." I glanced up to see Roy leaving Amanda at Dayshenay's house.

The two girls sat on the front porch rather than heading for the playground. Good. Their parents were taking things seriously. A few minutes later, Rose joined them, escorted by Danny. Safety in numbers, right?

Mags snapped her fingers in front of my face. "You need a plan in case you spot those boys again. Since Davis ordered you not to leave here, you can't very well follow them."

"Oh, I'd follow them regardless of orders." They couldn't get away again. I knew they weren't the ring leaders, but they were involved. First at Loren's and then the camper. Catch them, catch the boss.

"With Davis upping security around here, it'll be hard to do anything," Mags said.

"That's what I'm counting on." I'd also be watching the previous night's video feeds every morning. Super vigilance was going to be my motto.

Chapter Nine

The next morning, coffee in hand, I studied the surveillance videos. After ten p.m., no one roamed the property except for Mags and Larry. People were following orders. Maybe we would run this ring right out of our town. A quick glimpse at the clock had me scurrying to dress.

"Ann, the bus will be here in ten minutes." I hopped on one foot trying to put on my shoes. "The kids will already be gathering."

"I'm ready. You're the one who's running late." She smiled and headed for the front door, peering outside before stepping out. "Eric took Hershey with him."

"He usually does." I darted out the door toward the golf cart. Two minutes later, I parked under a tree and did a head count of the kids waiting at the community's entrance. All accounted for.

Actually, the children huddled together. Danny stood over them with a fierce look on his face. Sweet boy. He might have once stolen my laptop, but he'd turned his way around. I knew he'd do everything in his power to watch over the others.

I didn't let my guard down until they were all on the bus. "Now what?" I glanced at Ann. "They won't be back until three-thirty." With most of the adults at work and the kids at school, the place was a ghost town.

"What do you usually do?"

"Check emails, collect rent when it's due, sit around after driving the loop to see if any work needs doing, then I give the list to Roy."

"Then that's what we'll do."

It promised to be a long day. "I also need groceries."

"Order online and have them delivered."

I cut her a sharp glare. Obviously today was a day for rule following.

Groceries were first with a delivery time of three-fifteen. How was I supposed to be in two places at once? "You'll have to stay to accept the delivery, Ann. I'm going to be at the bus stop."

"We stay together." She glanced at her phone. "If we're at the gate, we'll see the delivery guy and can transfer the groceries to the back of the cart. Easy. Try all the tactics you want, CJ, but you aren't leaving Heavenly Acres."

"Fine." I stormed back outside, Caper in my arms, and left Ann to follow. Now that food was out of the way, I needed to make the rounds. I stashed my dog in the center of the seat. The minute Ann climbed in, I pressed the gas.

She yelped and grabbed the frame. "Not nice. Don't take Davis's orders out on me. I'm not the one in trouble."

"It really rips my skin that this followed me from Maui. The whole thing was a dark cloud over my honeymoon."

"Take another one when this is over."

"Easy for you to say. I'm not self-employed."

"Ha. You know Larry will give you anything you want."

True. After we'd found out about him and my mother being separated as children, he spoiled me. In fact, he'd known about me long before I met him, and he made sure I got the job as manager at Heavenly Acres.

We slowed at the home of Mrs. Wentworth. She bustled toward us wearing a house robe of pea green and rose pink.

"I've still got a leak." She hitched her chin. "That handyman has been here once. When is he coming back?"

"I'll check with him and get right back to you." I smiled. "Is there anything else?"

"Yes. You should be arrested for false advertising, calling this a safe and quiet place. It's been nothing but noise and drama since I arrived. I've lost count of how many times that detective has been at your place."

"Ma'am, Detective Davis is also a friend of ours. His presence doesn't necessarily mean anything is wrong."

"You trying to tell me that the bust over at the campground wasn't real? Or the warning flier handed to me?"

"You seem to know an awful lot about what goes

on around here." I leaned on the steering wheel deciding to try a different tactic to pacify the woman. "Perhaps we could use your talent to help us spot anyone who doesn't belong."

"I do like to be aware of my surroundings." She crossed her arms.

"Wonderful. You know where to find me if something strikes you strange." With the promise of checking with Roy, I drove away.

"Brilliant way of handling a troublesome woman," Ann said.

"Part of the job. Now, she feels important and might actually see something worthwhile." I stopped next to Roy's house where he carried a shovel to his cart.

"I need to replant a bush that's died," he said.

"I'm checking on the progress of the leak in number twenty."

"It's leaking again?" He frowned. "I told her not to shove so much stuff under her sink. She's moving the pipe. I'll figure something out. Build a cage around the thing if I have to."

"Thanks. Maybe build her a shelf somewhere else. Whatever makes her happy."

"There isn't a lot of space to do that in these houses, but I'll see what I can do. She won't let me in her bedroom or her bathroom. Keeps the doors closed at all times. The drawers under the stairs have locks on them. That is one strange woman indeed."

Locks? They'll cost money to repair once the woman moves on. I glanced at Ann. "Suspicious or am I reading too much into it?"

"Suspicious but most likely harmless. She

probably keeps the last twenty years of receipts in those drawers. Remember how many we found of your Grams's?"

True. Some people kept everything, it seemed. As for the locked doors, maybe she kept the cats locked up so they didn't escape.

We finished the loop and I drove to the chapel. It was time for a dusting.

I thought the last time anyone had been inside was my wedding until I spotted two sets of footprints in the aisle. "This looks like the same type of shoes Danny wears," I said, leaning down to study the zig-zag pattern. "Could this be our two mysterious young men?"

"Maybe." Ann snapped pictures of the prints. "We shouldn't disturb these right now. Cleaning can wait. Is there anywhere close by these men could hide out?"

I shook my head. "There are caves up the mountain but no buildings other than the ones at Heavenly Acres and the campground."

"Text Eric and have him look for tents or anything else a camper might sleep in. Those men are either close by or in town. If they're at a motel, they'll be found. Davis said he has officers going to each room."

Since trouble had come to me despite my resolve not to get involved, I itched to go into town and check out the motels myself. "They should check out every abandoned building while they're at it. All that will take too long."

"The FBI arrived this morning. They'll have help."

"How do you know that?" I narrowed my eyes.

"Davis keeps me up on what's happening."

"Why aren't you sharing this information with me?" I thought we were friends and partners.

"Sorry. I'm not used to sharing what I dig up for my clients."

"Since this concerns me, I want to know everything." After I checked the storage room and office, we left the chapel, and for the first time in a very long time, I locked the door. I wasn't going to give anyone an easy place to hide, and those rats had already been in a very special place of mine.

The campground was sadly empty during a time when all the sites should have been filled. I stopped at the place the camper had held the girl and exited the cart. Then, I walked to the site where the young men had camped and stepped into the woods. I had a strong suspicion he hadn't been using the restroom but was slinking over to the camper without being seen by his buddies.

In the firepit, I spotted the gold of a business card and used a stick to move around the ashes. Too much of the card had burned for me to know what it said. Using my fingertips, I picked it up and put it in my pocket. I moved to the woods, Ann behind me.

"What are we looking for?" she asked. "Anything in particular?"

"Something that links those who stayed here with those in the camper." Because one thing I did have was the rental information on the group from this site.

Ann laughed. "You manage to interfere in the investigation without leaving your own backyard."

"A girl does what a girl can." I stooped and picked up a complete gold and black card that read Timeless Pleasures. "What do you think this means? Prostitution and slavery have been around since the days of Moses. That could be what timeless means, right? I found a piece of a matching card in the firepit."

Ann shrugged. "Maybe those are handed out to interested men who show the card at the door and pay the fee?"

"Maybe. Which means at least one of the men from this site headed this way. One of them wasn't interested. What had the other three done?" Since we didn't find any more cards, I decided that three of them visiting the camper was a strong possibility.

We continued along the path until we saw the golf cart. "Good thinking," Ann said. "You should really be a detective. You have good instincts."

"Why didn't the police find these card remnants?"

"They didn't suspect anyone not at the camper is my guess. Why dig through the other firepits? It's the same as you finding those photos in the fridge. They looked in, saw stacked containers, and looked no further."

Sure, the force is small and overworked right now, but that kind of incompetence could get someone killed. "Let's turn these over to Davis. I need to print off the contact information."

Half an hour later, Ann and I sat at the picnic table outside my house and waited for Davis. Mags ran up as he arrived.

"Where have you been?" I asked, having

expected her to flag us down earlier and go with us on my rounds.

"The high school. I'm volunteering during lunch, so I can keep an eye on our girls while they are outside."

I grinned. "You're amazing."

"Okay, what do you have?" Davis cut off our conversation.

I slid a baggie with the two cards and rental information across the table while explaining my theory. "Have you seen other cards like these?"

He nodded. "There was a whole stack of them in the camper, and some of the men still had them in their pockets when we brought them to the station."

Oh. My shoulders slumped. "We didn't tell you anything new."

"Actually, you did. We have someone new to question." He tapped the baggy. "Good job. Hopefully, this is the break we need."

After he left, I turned to Mags. "Did you see anyone suspicious at the school? Any new students?"

She grinned. "Yes, I did, and there happens to be two very handsome young men who enrolled today. One dark, one light. I'm going to try and sneak a photo of them tomorrow."

Could they be the same ones we were looking for? It couldn't be that easy or they that stupid.

Chapter Ten

Ann was right. We intercepted the grocery delivery truck at the bus stop a few minutes before the bus arrived. After showing ID to prove we were who we said, we had the young man stash the bags in the back of the cart and waited for the kids to arrive home from school.

Thankfully, everyone who got on the bus that morning got off the bus that afternoon. I waved Danny over. "I heard two new guys started school."

"Subtle," Ann muttered.

"Yeah." Danny cocked his head. "They seem cool, why?"

"Just watching out for anyone new in town."

"I'll keep an eye on them, but they're actually a couple of geeks. Rose didn't give them a second look."

"They aren't handsome?"

He narrowed his eyes. "How would I know? One has an acne problem and the other wears thick glasses. I don't really look at guys, CJ."

Mags obviously had different taste in the opposite sex than today's teenage girls. I didn't think the new boys were the ones we were looking for.

"Don't worry, CJ. I'll let you know if anyone raises my radar." Danny rejoined the others and escorted all the girls to their homes before knocking on Rose's door. A few minutes later, they sat at the picnic table outside her chimney of a house and opened their schoolbooks.

Everything looked normal, so why did the nagging sense of something about to happen keep pricking at me? We were taking every possible precaution. Short of locking everyone up, there wasn't anything more we could do except not let down our guard.

Ann searched the internet for newcomers to the area while I put away the groceries. "I doubt I'll find anything. Don't think these people will use their real identities."

I agreed. "I'd like to go into town and see if I can spot Manu or the fake Landon. Eric and I are the only ones who have seen the two men's faces, at least here on the mainland."

"They might not have come to the mainland. I'm sure there are pieces of their ring in every state." She glanced at her vibrating cellphone. "It's Davis." She answered and listened quietly, her expression serious. When the call ended, she glanced my way. "Another girl is missing. She never made it home after school."

"Not a runaway this time?" My heart dropped.

"They don't think so. A good girl, good grades, never in trouble." She slammed her laptop closed. I recognized the look on her face. My friend was devising a plan. One that might go against Davis's orders.

"Uh oh." Eric paused in the doorway. "What's going on? You two are up to something."

"Another girl went missing," Ann said.

"And?" He set his wallet and keys on a shelf by the front door.

"Nothing. Yet." She pushed to her feet. "Would I pass as a teenager?"

I studied my tall, buxom blonde friend. "Nope. A prostitute maybe with the right clothes, but definitely not a teenager."

"Yeah, that's what I thought. Too bad you're so well known around here."

"I cannot believe the two of you are thinking like Mags. You want someone to be bait."

"It's the only way to flush the men out and stop girls from being taken." Ann's famous cop mask fell into place. The one where no one could read her thoughts or change her mind.

"Who are you going to get?" I asked, setting a pan of water on the stove to boil.

"I'm going to talk to Davis about using a female undercover cop." She grabbed her purse. "Don't leave the house. I'll eat when I return." She rushed out the door, locking it behind her.

Eric stepped up behind me and kissed the back of my neck. "Spaghetti?"

I nodded, closing my eyes and leaning into him. "I had groceries delivered today. How did things go with Milton?"

Chuckling, he stepped back. "He's not an

outdoorsman. He's afraid of spiders, of which this state has plenty, and he complained of the heat and humidity all day. Hopefully, he can return to his real job soon, or I'm going to strangle him."

"At least you get to leave the community." I broke spaghetti noodles in half and dropped them into the water. "I'm not exactly sure how an undercover cop will work when no one has any idea who the men are or how they're luring the girls. Anyone hanging around the school would be noticed. The girl today never made it home, which makes it sound like a snatch and grab. None of it makes any sense."

"I agree. On Maui the ring was organized. The girls followed until the right time came." He poured two glasses of tea from the fridge. "I'm glad you aren't allowed to leave, CJ. People died on Maui."

"You leave."

"I'm doing my job. You'd be snooping, something you aren't very discreet about."

I shrugged. My husband wasn't wrong. When I bit into something, it was hard to shake me loose. I'd concentrate my efforts on keeping those in the community safe. If trouble came too close, all rules were going to be thrown out.

Once supper was prepared, we carried everything outside, letting the dogs lie under the table while we ate. Ann hadn't arrived by the time we finished or by the time we sat, drinks in hand, in lawn chairs by the lake's edge.

I typed Davis a quick text asking if she'd arrived and if so, when she left. Before I pressed send, Ann's car parked behind mine.

"I was getting worried." I glared up at her.

"Sorry. The FBI guys were kind of a pain, not liking that Davis and I were insistent on using someone as bait. They finally agreed and said they'd take it from there and infiltrate someone into the high school as a student."

"Doesn't sound like enough time to make you gone so long." I narrowed my eyes.

She avoided my gaze. "I might have done a little investigating on my own."

"No fair."

"I'm not ordered to stay once Eric returns home. Sorry."

I shoved aside my disappointment. "Did you find out anything?"

"Two young men who match the description of the two visiting Loren just checked out of the local motel. No forwarding address, but I doubt they left town. There are several outlying buildings, vacated businesses, barns, etc., where they could hide. It will take a while to search them all."

"Nobody knows the area as well as Eric does."

"Yes, and that's not all." She handed me a photo. "CJ Turley, meet CJ Turley."

I glanced at a woman who could be my twin. "What's this?"

"The undercover agent. The feds said since you always meddle in police investigations, why not go along with what you're known for? The bad guys will expect you to meddle. This CJ will be staying in your grandmother's house and attending the high school as a student."

I frowned, amazed at the resemblance. "They

actually think this will work?”

“No, but they do believe it will draw those in the ring into the open in an attempt to come after you, or rather her.” She rubbed her hands together. “Which means, that leaves us free to do some snooping. All eyes will be on CJ number two.”

I cut a glance toward my thoughtful husband. His gaze remained on the lake as he processed Ann’s idea. After several agonizing moments, he spoke, “It might work except for one thing.”

“What?” Ann and I said in unison.

“If these men have been watching CJ, they’ll know she has another woman with her at all times.”

“I wouldn’t if I were at the school,” I said. “I’d be hanging out with kids. How can we spread the word around that I’m pretending to be a teen?”

“We won’t have to.” Ann shook her head. “They’re watching the school. They know what you look like, CJ—not the name you’re enrolling under, by the way—you’re Carla Turner. Anyway, they’ll recognize you. Trust me when I say that everyone involved was most likely given a photo of you by those goons on Maui.”

It was moments like these that made being a well-known snoop not so great. I wanted to suggest Danny and Rose befriend this Carla, but that could put them in harm’s way. “We need to let the students from Heavenly Acres know to stay away from Carla.”

“Good point.” Eric stood and held out his hand. “Let’s let them all know to steer clear and keep quiet. It wouldn’t take much to blow the agent’s cover.”

We went to the Olson home, the Flower home, and the Washington home where all the teens agreed to keep our secret. In fact, they seemed thrilled to be a part of it all. I could only pray none of them would end up as collateral damage in the FBI's infiltration of the school.

If Carla were taken, it wouldn't be for trafficking. No, she'd be targeted for death. These people needed to be found before this happened or more girls disappeared. I'd also like to find out what happened to Loren. It wasn't going to be anything good.

We returned home, and Eric pulled some maps out of a desk drawer and spread them on the coffee table. "No one goes out without a plan. Milton and I can take anything in the woods or further up the mountain. The two of you, along with Mags—or she'll scream bloody murder and give us away—will take the town." He uncapped a red marker. "I cannot believe I'm doing this." He circled a spot on the map. "These warehouses along the river are the perfect hiding place. Not only for kidnappers but also for their victims. Over here." He tapped another spot, "It's a run-down motel that's been out of business for over ten years. Don't forget to check RV parks and truck stops."

I glanced up from the map. "You know an awful lot about this."

"Ever since Maui, I've been doing some research. Sporting events, truck stops, rest stops, you name it, trafficking is there. I'm sure the police are also looking in those places. Maybe you ladies would want to focus more on vacant houses in town. It'll be safer than the more remote places."

"We'll be careful." I put a hand on his arm. "I promise. We need to do our part since…well, this followed us here. With two CJs running around, we'll keep the criminals confused. They'll make a mistake."

"There's no saying it wouldn't have come to our town anyway." He handed me the map of the town. "Keep your taser and cell phone with you at all times. Follow Ann's orders. Don't let Mags get crazy." He chuckled, resting his forehead against mine. "I couldn't go on without you, Clarice Josephine."

"Nor I you."

"We could run away and hide until this is all over."

"You know neither one of us could do that with a clear conscience." I raised my gaze and cupped his face.

"You're right. Let's find these guys and try to have a normal married life, okay?"

"Sounds perfect."

Ann cleared her throat. "I hate to break up this little love fest, but someone is roaming around the campground."

We bolted to our feet and ran for the gator, both dogs on our heels. "We can't take them," I said. "They'll bark and give us away."

"Hold on." Eric locked them in the house, then hopped in the driver's seat and sped toward the campground.

I hated sitting in the backseat, but since I was the only one not carrying a gun, I kept my mouth shut and held on for dear life.

Chapter Eleven

The gator hit a large pothole in our wild ride toward the campground. I bounced and almost fell over the side. "Slow down."

Eric hit the brakes. "Stay down, stay quiet, and be prepared to call Davis."

I knew the drill. I also knew I was the weakest link in the chain. Unless directly faced with danger, I had no problems following orders. Well, that's a lie, isn't it? Okay, I *tried* to follow orders.

With Eric leading the way and Ann behind me, we sped down the path that circled the lake until we reached the trailer where Mr. Robinson, the man who had run the campgrounds when I'd first been hired, once stood. The trailer was gone, as was the man, but the storage building remained. We took shelter behind it as clouds covered the rising moon.

"What exactly did you see?" Eric whispered.

"A flashlight." Ann pointed. "Over there."

I strained my eyes but couldn't see anything until the clouds parted and the full moon lit up the area like early morning. Tough luck for the man sneaking around.

He glared at the sky, then turned his attention back to the ground. What could he possibly be hoping to find? There couldn't be anything left after the authorities and Ann and I combed the area.

"What are we going to do?" I asked.

"Wait and see what he does," Eric answered. "If he's up to no good, we don't want to scare him off."

The man moved from camp site to camp site, shining his flashlight on the ground in a large sweeping motion. Since he didn't concentrate on the site where the camper had been, I doubted he was one of the traffickers. So what was he looking for?

"I don't think he's a bad guy." I straightened.

"I agree." Ann stepped from our shelter. "Eric, find out what he's looking for."

"Excuse me, sir." Eric stepped into the road. "I'm Park Ranger Drake. May I help you?"

The man whirled, blinding me with his flashlight. "You scared me. Let me see some identification."

Eric approached slowly, holding out his badge. The man studied it, then nodded. "I know I'm not supposed to be here. I saw the notice at the entrance, but before the police closed the camp and sent us all away, my wife lost her wedding ring. This is the only place we haven't looked."

Thank goodness it was nothing more. "We'll help you look. Which site were you in?"

"106, but we took regular walks around this loop, always walking on the right side, my wife between me and the edge."

The chances of finding the ring were slim, but we

might get lucky. We formed a straight line keeping a few feet away from each other in hopes of seeing the ring if the person in front of us missed it.

Halfway around the circle, I spotted something sparkling in the grass in the gleam of my light. Not a ring but a tiny gold cross necklace. I picked it up and slipped it into my pocket. Someone might have reported it missing on the lost-and-found section of the campground website.

"Find anything?" The man glanced over his shoulder.

"Nope." I smiled. Since it wasn't his wife's ring, it wasn't anything he needed to know about. "Not yet."

We completed the loop and found nothing more. Not even another Timeless Pleasures business card. The campground was swept clean.

"Sorry, sir. We tried. Maybe the ring wasn't lost here after all," I said.

"Maybe not. Thanks for your help." He headed for the entrance.

"What did you find?" Eric asked.

I should have known he'd picked up on me finding something. My husband didn't miss much. "A cross necklace. I didn't need him claiming what wasn't his. I'll try to find out who lost it."

Ann froze. "The girl who went missing today wore a gold cross necklace. He wasn't looking for a ring." She broke into a sprint after the man. Eric and I followed.

We were too late. The red taillights of a car speeding away was all we could see when we reached the entrance.

"They'd brought her through the campground. Why?" I glanced at Eric. "There's nothing here."

"We're missing something." He bit the inside of his cheek and paced the area.

I patrolled the campsites every day until no more campers were allowed. What could we possibly be missing? Nothing but trees, cement pads, picnic tables, and restrooms.

"I'm calling Davis," Ann said. When she hung up, she told us we were to go home, and that the FBI would send a team out in the morning to go over the sites again, and someone would retrieve the necklace I'd found and show it to the missing girl's mother.

"Maybe we should stake out the sites," I said after we returned home. "There has to be a reason the girl was taken through there today. And when would they have been able to do so without us seeing them?"

"I saw their flashlight." Ann shrugged. "During the day, there would've been no need for one."

"We would have heard a vehicle, though, right?" I glanced from her to Eric.

"Not unless the wind was blowing in the right direction." Eric stopped and glanced at the dark silhouette of the mountain. "I think they're hiding the girls somewhere up there until they can move them."

"The same tunnels the drug people used?"

"Maybe. I'll mention them to the feds tomorrow and let them check them out. They were supposed to be blocked so no one had access anymore." He unlocked the front door to the house and let the dogs out to do their business before retiring for the night.

Where else could someone go if they went

through the campgrounds? "The chapel. They're using the chapel."

Eric and Ann turned to stare, then we raced again for the gator. Once we reached the chapel, I turned the knob on the front door. It swung open at my push. "I locked this."

"Get back." Ann stepped in front of me and pulled her gun. "The footprints are still here in the dust, two heading in that direction and now two coming this way. Same size, same print. Where can someone hide?"

"The office for any visiting pastor and the storage room are the only places. Neither are very big, but they can hold a few people." I headed for the office and unlocked the door before turning on the light. "Someone's been here. How did they get a key to the chapel, and why are they hanging around so close?"

"Because the town is overrun with feds?" Ann entered the room, snapping photos of blankets and empty food and water containers. "Now, they'll have to find another place to hide."

I unlocked the storage room next. The window had been broken letting me know how the men had gained entrance. A pair of denim-clad legs and a foul odor greeted me. "Found Loren." He'd been shot between the eyes at close range. "I guess he isn't one of them after all."

"He's one of us."

I shrieked and whirled to see Ann and Eric with guns pointed at a man in a black suit. "Tell me you're FBI."

"I am." He showed us his badge. "Agent Tyson. Loren was an undercover agent. He befriended the two young men who are the lures for the girls. How they're luring them, we don't know yet. We've been looking for Loren since his disappearance. We didn't expect to find him alive."

"How did you know we were here?" Eric hadn't lowered his weapon.

"You weren't at home and I followed the tracks. It wasn't difficult."

"Who do you think killed him? The young men?"

"I doubt it." He exhaled heavily. "You have a necklace?"

I handed it to him and gave a description of the man we'd tried to help. "Loren was moved here recently. Ann and I were here just a couple of days ago and the body wasn't. Why bring the body here and not hide it in the woods?"

Agent Tyson's sharp gaze focused on me. "Because by putting him here, they're warning you. I'll have someone come for the body. Be careful, Miss Turley." He strode from the chapel, his warning hanging in the air like a thundercloud.

I really hadn't done anything…yet. But these people thought I knew something, and they would be coming for me. Well, come on. I'd be waiting. I might be small, but I wasn't weak or a coward.

Warnings had become a regular part of my life, it seemed. Sleep didn't take long to arrive, and I woke the next morning feeling refreshed. As horrible as the undercover agent's death was, it did set things in motion which meant we were closer to ending it all and seeing justice done.

"You're as bad as Mags," Eric said as we sat down with our coffee. "You look energized, almost excited."

"Only because we're finally getting somewhere. I wasn't going to get involved. You know that. I can't help it when it comes to me."

"It always comes to you. Try to cover that crazy mane of hair today and wear sunglasses. There's no need to make identifying you any easier than it needs to be."

Ann joined us. "Mags and I will do the same. In fact, I'll be dressed as a man."

"Better do some heavy-duty strapping on that chest of yours," Mags said, coming up behind us. "I'll make myself appear older. No one will recognize us."

"I thought we wanted these guys to know there were two CJ's roaming around."

"Changed my mind," Ann said. "They're too close. Let them focus on CJ number two. We need to concentrate on where they hold the girls. The warnings will still come, but they'll come for whatever the other gal does. We need to let them think that it's undercover cops living in this house. I want you to pack suitcases and drive to your Grams's house. We'll change into our disguises there and slip out the back door."

"You must have been up all night thinking this over." It was a good plan until I thought a little deeper on the subject. "What about the dogs?" Obviously, that was the one kink in her plan. "I prefer keeping Caper with me."

"Same here," Eric said. "Hershey is a great warning system."

Ann sighed. "I have no idea how to proceed from

here."

"You could always dye the dogs' hair," Mags said. "People do it all the time."

"That won't work for a lab." Eric frowned. "She'll still look like a lab except a different color."

"I could disguise Caper easy enough, I guess." My poor dog would pout for a week. "Those guys aren't stupid enough to fall for this. They might for the CJ at the high school, but why would three undercover cops stay in my house without me?"

Ann rubbed her face. "I must be tired. You're right. Eric and I will disguise ourselves. You remain yourself. No, Eric needs to be himself. Oh, I've messed this up."

"Bummer." Mags got up. "I was looking forward to having to stay with y'all in that big old house of yours. Guess I'll be myself, too. See you a little later."

"CJ is the only one not using a disguise. I want the guys to think she's surrounded by protection. There will be a blonde woman and a pretend husband with CJ number two." Ann stood. "I think we've got rid of the wrinkles now. If a blonde woman is with CJ number two, it stands to reason the feds might appoint protection on the real CJ, right? You know what? Forget it. My brain is too fuzzy to think this through."

"How long has it been since you've had a good night's sleep?" Eric asked.

"Since I moved in here."

She did take her job seriously. "The fake me needs a dog."

"Darn these dogs! They're making everything

more difficult. Do you have to go everywhere with them?"

Eric and I said yes in unison. "They're our babies," I said. "One wouldn't leave their child behind, would they?"

"I was on the phone a long time with Davis last night coming up with this plan. He's going to lose the top of his head when I bring up the dogs."

"I'm sure you can find something similar to Caper and Hershey at the pound." I pushed to my feet. "If we're going to start today, I need to shed these shorts and tee shirt. I'm not going into any abandoned buildings unless my legs are protected with jeans." I glanced up as Milton arrived. "Looks like your partner is here." I raised my face for Eric to kiss me. "Be careful."

"You, too." He motioned for Hershey to follow and sprinted for the gator.

I met Ann's gaze. "Let's get this day started." Hopefully, tomorrow's plans wouldn't need so much unraveling in order to make sense. "Tonight, you need to take something to help you sleep. You're of no use to any of us as confused as you are this morning."

Chapter Twelve

I kept a watchful eye on Ann as she drove us into town. Dark shadows under her eyes confirmed her lack of sleep. I felt bad for not having noticed sooner. I peered closer at her face. Maybe it was more than a lack of sleep. She'd been tired before but never this cranky. "Are you feeling sick?"

She cut me a sideways glance. "No. Why?"

"You don't look good."

"Just tired." She pulled into a parking spot in front of the drugstore. "I need something to keep me alert."

"Coffee?"

"Don't take any of those energy drinks," Mags said from the backseat. "They'll give you a heart attack."

"Did you eat anything when you were in town yesterday?" I tilted my head. "Because you have the look of someone whose blood sugar is crashing."

"Yes, I ate something. Had something to drink, too. I stopped at the diner."

I glanced over my shoulder at Mags, then back at Ann. "Did you leave your food and drink unattended?" The more I studied her face, the more she resembled Mags the time someone had poisoned her.

"I went to the bath…oh for crying out loud. What a rookie mistake. How could I forget this town is not as innocent as it appears?"

"Well, you aren't dead, so it wasn't a fatal dose." Mags patted her shoulder.

"That's because Davis called me, and I didn't get to finish my meal." She pounded the steering wheel. "What an idiot."

Mags patted her shoulder again. "At least now you know that you weren't losing your mind coming up with such a crazy plan."

Ann glared in the rearview mirror. "Davis helped me come up with that plan."

"Did he?" Mags arched a brow.

"Sort of. I did most of it while trying to sleep. Oh, I don't know how much he came up with." She sighed and cut the engine. "Let's start checking out these buildings. Whatever I was given will work its way through my system eventually."

I wouldn't be eating or drinking anything I didn't prepare myself. With Ann out of the way, I would be virtually unprotected. Whoever had slipped her the drug or poison would try again. "Maybe Davis needs to send us another person. Not to replace you but to help."

If looks could kill, the one Ann sent me would have struck me dead. "I can protect you."

"Yes, but who's going to protect you? It's not

that you're incapable, just human, and my friend. I don't want anything to happen to you." I shoved my hair under a baseball cap and slipped on a pair of oversized sunglasses.

"Awesome," Mags said. "You look like yourself, but only if someone looks close. All eyes will be on the CJ enrolling in school. Nighttime is when the focus transfers back to you."

"Oh, goody." I stepped onto the sidewalk, setting Caper on the ground and holding firmly to her leash. "The first place is only a block away. An old video rental store turned trophy shop, now vacant. It used to be a favorite hangout for the homeless."

I cupped my hands around my eyes and peered through the grimy window. It didn't look as if anyone had been inside in a long time. No footprints in the inches of dirt. "Want to look around back?"

"Yes." Ann led the way. "No stone unturned and all that."

"Aren't we going inside?" Mags frowned.

"No, we're only to see if we find a lead, then report it to Davis. Under no circumstances are we to enter a building or confront a suspect unless absolutely necessary."

"That takes a lot of fun out of things." Mags peered over her sunglasses. "Where to next?"

Ann wouldn't like the next option because we couldn't check it out without going inside. "The abandoned mall."

"Seriously?" Ann rolled her eyes. "You pulled that one up on purpose."

"It's on the map." I showed her where Eric had circled and put a number two. "My husband numbered them as he thought they might be prioritized as hiding places until the people could be moved. There're probably a hundred stores in that mall. It's supposed to be torn down soon, which makes it perfect for the ring's purposes."

"And will use up our entire day." Grouchy Ann led us back to the car and drove us to the mall on the outskirts of town.

If I had my way, I'd hold everything off until the next day and take Ann home to get some sleep.

We passed the high school on our way, and I glanced to where the kids gathered in the courtyard. "There I am." It was weird seeing someone who looked so much like me hanging out with teenagers and pretending to be one of them. I don't think I ever acted like a typical teenager. Too shy and too many responsibilities.

A dark van sat across the street. I ducked low in my seat and glanced over to see a stony-faced man in dark glasses watching the school. FBI or predator? I sent Davis a text. Let him worry about the van that stood out like a crow among snow white doves. I really was trying to stay a safe distance away from harm, especially now with Ann having come so close to possible death.

At the mall, she glanced down at Caper. "Since we're going inside, I now wish we had a bigger dog."

"She'll let us know if we aren't alone."

"I've seen her attack someone's ankle before," Mags said. "It provided a distraction. Don't knock the dog because she's small. Look at CJ. She's come up close and personal with men twice her size and talked them to death."

I laughed remembering the man who had marched me through the woods with orders to kill me. He couldn't wait to get away from me after I talked the entire hike. "We use what talents we have."

"Right now, you need to keep your wits about you and your Taser handy." Ann stared at the broken chain on the ground. "Someone has been here recently."

"Druggies?" Mags widened her eyes.

"I'd take them over the ones we're really looking for."

"Want me to call Davis?" I asked.

She shook her head. "We need more information before we take an already overworked detective from what he's currently involved in. And we need to be quiet. If we see anything suspicious inside that points to someone other than homeless or drug users, we leave and then let Davis or the feds know."

I agreed. A handful of people could only do so much, and at least half of those were watching over the other CJ. The three of us needed to do what we could to help. There. A guilt-free reason to get involved. Lord, keep us safe.

Ann entered the building first, Mags and I at the same time staying just a couple of feet behind our Amazon friend. I stood and listened for a scuffle, anything to alert us that we were not alone. When none came, Ann motioned to our right.

"We'll stay to the right, checking each store," she whispered. "We move fast and quiet. If I say run, don't ask any questions. Just get outside as fast as possible."

Mags and I nodded. I seriously didn't think Ann would have to tell us twice.

Caper, nose to the ground, pulled against her leash in a desire to have free rein. If I let her go, I'd have to chase her down, and that act might put me in a bad situation. I'd keep an eye on her body language to determine whether or not she smelled something to be concerned about.

Some of the stores had iron gates locked into place letting us bypass searching them. A broken skylight overhead helped us see without the aid of flashlights.

I remembered going to the mall many times with Grams before she became too ill to enjoy the outings anymore. It broke my heart to see the place in such disrepair. But, so many people shopped online now or headed to the bigger cities that the smaller malls couldn't compete.

We turned the corner to another section of the X-shaped interior of the building and arrived at the restrooms. Ann held up her fist for us to stop and put a finger to her lips.

Caper sniffed along the edge of the door, tail wagging, then glanced up at me.

Ann pushed the door open. Lying on the edge of the sink was a bright pink press-on nail, the type a young girl would purchase from the drugstore. Since it wasn't covered in dust, it didn't take a wise woman to know the nail hadn't been there long.

"Time to go," Ann said.

"We don't know it belongs to one of the missing teens," I said.

Caper yanked her leash free and darted away.

With a hoarse order to come back, I took off after her. "Caper."

"CJ," Ann called. "We have to go."

"Not without my dog," I forced the words past a whisper. "She's onto something. Trust me." Increasing my speed, my feet pounded loudly in the cavernous space. If anyone was there, they knew we were coming now. Caper raced past the food courts and through an empty department store. As she made her way nimbly up the non-running escalator, I almost gave up. By the time I reached the top, my breath came in pants. I stopped and bent over, balancing my hands on my knees to catch my breath. Ann raced ahead of me, Mags stopping next to me, also having trouble catching her breath.

"Girl, I'm thirty years older than you, and you're in as bad of shape as I am. You need to hit the gym." She clapped her hand on my shoulder. "Come on."

I forced myself forward, praying we wouldn't run into any bad guys. I was going to wring my dog's neck for running off. She'd better find something good.

Caper stopped at the department store office door and added scratching to her barking. I grabbed her leash and pulled her back as Ann tried the door.

"Locked."

"Something is in there. Caper wouldn't act like this otherwise. You'll have to break it open."

"With what?"

"Shoot the lock," Mags said. "It works in the movies."

"This isn't the movies. If someone is in there, the bullet could ricochet and hit them." Ann shook her head. "There. That iron clothes rack. Maybe I can jimmy the door open with the top bar."

Mags rolled the rack toward her, then Ann removed the bar and slammed it into the lock. After the third time, the door swung open, and we stared into the frightened eyes of three bound and gagged girls.

"Caper, you found a true treasure this time," I said as my pup licked the tears off the face of one of the girls.

Chapter Thirteen

While Mags called Davis and Ann stood guard, I searched the room for something to cut the bindings around the girls' hands and feet. As I removed their gags, I put a finger to my lips. If someone didn't yet know we were here, which seemed highly unlikely, we didn't need to alert them. "You're okay now. We won't leave you." I jerked upright at a thud downstairs.

One of the girls clapped a hand over her mouth and scooted closer to the one next to her. As more than one pair of feet thundered toward us, I wrapped my arms around the girls and held on tight while Caper barked.

Ann planted her feet shoulder-width apart, gun held out in front of her. Mags clutched her Taser. We were all a formidable sight…to a mouse maybe.

"Don't shoot." Davis's head appeared at the top of the escalator. "Let's move these girls safely out of here. Good job, ladies, although I asked that you not enter any buildings."

"We couldn't search a place this size without going inside." I held out my hand to pull one girl to her feet and caught a glimpse of something shiny and purple. I bent to pick up a string of sequins. Left behind from an outfit no longer available for purchase? I slipped it into my pocket. It would make a cute collar for Caper.

A van waited near the mall's entrance, and we climbed inside. "I'll see you at the station." Davis closed the doors and pounded that we were free to go.

"Can you tell us your names?" I leaned forward, wanting desperately to erase the look of fear from their eyes. Maybe if I persuaded them to talk, they'd relax a little. "And how long have you been missing?"

"I'm Ashley. They took me after school yesterday."

"I'm Carla. I'm not from here. They brought me here last week."

"Rosa. Same."

"How long were you in the mall?"

Ashley shrugged. "Since last night, maybe. They said they would have to keep moving us until it was time for our debut. I heard them say someone kept messing up their plans."

I glanced at Ann. These people didn't sound very organized to me. "That would be us messing things up." I smiled, glad to be a troublemaker for a change. "Are there more girls?"

All three nodded, but only Ashley spoke. "They keep us in small groups to make us easier to handle and transport."

"Did they, uh—"

"No. One of them said we were selected for someone more important."

Thank goodness for that. "Can you describe who took you? I know this is a lot of questions, and the police will ask the same ones and more, but if we're going to help keep this from happening to other girls, we need all the details you can remember."

"I understand. One of the guys was black, Devon, the other white, Billy. Both really cute." Tears sprang to her eyes. "They just grabbed me, but they usually meet a girl online, then ask her to meet in person." She lowered her voice. "They're desperate."

I exchanged another look with Ann. "What do you mean?"

"They seemed scared. I think they might have stolen Carla and Rosa from someone else."

As in going into business for themselves? A couple of boys barely out of their teens? This could not end well for them. We might have a war arriving in our town. "Do you know where they stay?"

"No. They took us to a motel at first, then the mall. Rosa said she heard big trucks once. They always move us at night. Stay with us." Ashley gripped my hand as we arrived at the station. "At least until my mom comes."

I glanced at Ann and Mags who nodded. "We'll stay with you." At least until Davis ran us out.

A female agent escorted us to a room with a large oval table. "There's water. The bathroom is through that door. I'll see if I can find you some food, and we'll contact your parents."

The girls converged on the water cooler as if they

hadn't drunk anything in a long time. Maybe they hadn't. The young men might not be smart enough to realize they needed to keep their captives healthy for them to be worth anything on the market.

The agent returned with a box of doughnuts which the girls devoured. Caper went from one to the other begging for scraps and eliciting smiles from the girls. Sometimes you just needed a sweet dog to make things right in your world. While they ate, I wrote down everything they'd told me—names, descriptions, and the like.

I wanted to catch these guys and slap them silly. Not only were they scum by acting as lures for young girls, but they were also extremely stupid, going up against far more experienced criminals.

As expected, Davis and Agent Tyson asked us to leave while they questioned the girls. I hugged the three of them, gave Davis an exasperated look, wiggled the page I'd written on at him, and led the way from the room. Waving that paper was like a red flag. He'd be by the house later to find out what I knew and to compare notes.

I stopped short at the sight of Ann's car in the parking lot. "How did that get here?"

"I texted Larry." Mags grinned. "After I told him what we'd found, and that the girls wanted us to stay with them, he was more than happy to have it dropped off. Now we can go back right away and figure out how to catch those punks. You probably noticed I was unusually quiet since we found the girls."

"Yes, I did." I tilted my head.

"I was soaking it all in, listening to everything,

and now I have a plan." Head high, she marched to the car and slid into the backseat.

"Guess we'll find out the plan later," I mumbled, climbing into the front passenger seat with Caper. My pup deserved a super special treat for her part in the girls' rescue. We might not have found them without her.

Ann had been quiet, too, but that wasn't as unusual for her. "Are you feeling better?" I asked.

"Yes." Her brow furrowed. "If I understand Ashley correctly, there are more small groups of girls hidden in the area. Why here? Why this town?" She glanced at me. "Because of you? That doesn't make sense."

"Maybe it's because we're small, our police force is small, people are trusting…" I shrugged, agreeing it couldn't be just because of what I'd seen on Maui. "Landon knew about me, which means he knows the sort of town I live in. They probably thought things would be easy for them. I'm happy to prove them wrong."

"I think you're right. This ring thought they could get away with something here. They were wrong." Ann pulled onto the highway and headed for home.

At the house, I went inside and filled a tray with tea and glasses of ice before joining the others at the picnic table outside. "Let's hear your plan, Mags." I poured tea into the glasses.

"I'm going to make up fliers with a drawing and description of our two young hoodlums and plaster them all over town. They won't be able to take a step without someone snitching."

"Davis will already have a BOLO out on them,"

I said.

"But he won't go to the same lengths that we can. He doesn't have the manpower. The three of us will go into every business, tack a flier on every light post and telephone pole, at the high school—everywhere we can. It will take us all day tomorrow, maybe longer. It's a good plan. I know it is. Plus, it's a great way to be out and about snooping. We might find more girls or even the punks themselves."

That was a stretch, but handing out fliers might actually flush the boys out. They obviously weren't experts in their rotten choice of a profession. It was worth a try.

"We'll still have to be careful," Ann said. "And we can't focus all of our attention on the two young guys. There are more experienced traffickers out there, and they'll be carrying a grudge. Not only against the two fools who betrayed them but us for getting in the way."

"We can't stop," I said. "We're actually making a difference. A far bigger difference than ever before. We're saving children."

"I didn't say to stop. I said we need to be careful. Finding those girls today, seeing them tied up, made this more real than ever."

"I say no eating out, no drinking anything that we didn't pour ourselves, no going anywhere alone, no going out after dark, not that it matters," Mags nodded. "Girls are being taken during the day, but we aren't as valuable. When they come for us, it will be a blitz attack."

I agreed and glanced at the mountain rising behind the houses. I prayed Eric was being safe.

There were a lot of places for an ambush up there, and the best way to get to me was through those I cared about.

"Don't worry." Ann smiled. "Milton will watch your man's back. Remember, he used to be my partner. I know what he's capable of."

I nodded. Milton had to help keep me from being killed once—a job he hadn't liked since I tended to be on the less careful side when getting close to finding the bad guy. But, he'd taken good care of me despite myself.

"After caring for Grams on my own for so many years, it's hard to relinquish control to someone else." I wrapped my hands around my sweating glass. "It's hard to believe anyone can keep my friends and family safer than I can."

"Don't forget the Big Man upstairs." Mags pointed heavenward. "You've kept Him very busy over the last year. He hasn't given up yet."

"True." I laughed. "I definitely keep my guardian angel busy. Poor thing probably has stooped shoulders and gray hair by now."

Speaking of gray hair. I glanced up to see Mrs. Wentworth hurry past on her way home. She clutched a shopping bag in each hand. I couldn't be sure, because she wasn't the friendliest woman to begin with, but the sharp gaze she sent my way didn't give me any warm fuzzies. I hope Roy figured out how to make her happy regarding her leaking sink. The last thing I needed right now was a disgruntled resident.

The woman continued her march to her house and sent me another glare before entering number twenty. "Why is it that there is always at least one person around who doesn't like me?" I glanced at my friends.

"No idea," Mags said. "You aren't exactly intimidating. Now me, on the other hand, can put the fear of God in people. Want me to find out what put a burr in that woman's bobby sock?"

I laughed. "No, leave her be. I'll stop by there in the morning."

Chapter Fourteen

After much admiration from my husband, I drifted into a deep sleep of self-satisfaction. While we hadn't stopped the traffickers, we'd saved three more girls, and that warmed my heart.

"You look pleased with yourself this morning." Eric rolled onto his side and smiled down at me.

"I'm very pleased. Today, we get to flush out some rats." I gave him a quick kiss. "What are your plans?"

"Still searching the mountain, grid by grid. If they're up there, which I'm starting to doubt, we'll find them."

"Leave no rock unturned." I kissed him again and climbed out of bed. "Do you have time for coffee?"

"Yes, please." He carried his uniform to the bathroom on the other side of the house. "I'll make omelets."

"Yummy." He made the best, filled with ham, cheese, and mushrooms. I started the coffee, fed all three fur babies, and then stood at the window to watch my little community come to life.

Danny walked the other children to the bus stop, keeping a close eye on the girls in particular. I smiled at the ferocity on his face as they passed anyone daring to get too close.

After a delicious breakfast for three, I tied the sequin ribbon around Caper's neck and joined Ann outside. "I need to check on Mrs. Wentworth first. Do you mind?"

"Not at all. You still have a job to do."

It being a pleasant spring morning, we waited with the children at the bus stop until they were safely on the bus, then walked to house number twenty. The door opened before I could knock.

"What?" Mrs. Wentworth gently scooted a cat away from the door with her foot.

"I'm checking to make sure your leak has been fixed." I forced a smile to my face.

"Yes." She started to close the door.

I stuck my foot in the way. "May I see for myself? You seemed upset last night as you carried your bags home."

"You're a nosy woman." She narrowed her eyes, then stepped back. "Suit yourself, but make it quick. I've things to do."

"I'll only be a few seconds." I headed to the small galley kitchen and looked under the sink. Paper towels, toilet paper, a stack of paper cups, cleaning supplies, and a pile of paper plates completely filled the small space. A small metal cage covered the pipes to prevent anyone from forcing too much in and pressing against them. Good job, Roy. I straightened to see Mrs. Wentworth staring at the ribbon around

Caper's neck. "Looks good. I doubt you'll have any more problems."

Her gaze hardened as she switched her attention to me. "Hopefully not." She opened the front door and ushered me outside where Ann waited before slamming the door closed.

Definitely not a friendly person, this woman. I shook off her bad attitude and headed with Ann to her car where Mags waited.

"I've done what I think is a good drawing of those punks." Her voice lowered as if she was trying to imitate Dirty Harry. "Take a look."

"Wow. These are actually very good. I didn't know you were an artist." The drawings looked very much like the two young men we were looking for. "I don't think you should put *Wanted: Dead or Alive*, though. This isn't the wild west."

She smirked. "We can have the photo shop take that part out. I had fun writing it, and I've scribbled a picture off and on over the years." She took her usual place in the back seat.

At the copy business, the young man behind the counter studied the drawings. His brow furrowed. "Seems like I've seen these guys before. They the ones kidnapping the girls?"

Ann nodded. "We suspect they're two of them, anyway. How long until the copies are done?"

"Fifteen minutes. You can put one in the window when they're finished. I'll print them for free." He took the pages to a large copy machine. "I can't charge for something this important."

"You're a good boy," Mags said. "You call us if you remember where you've seen them." She scribbled our phone numbers on the back of one of his business cards.

Ann snatched the card up. "Call the police, not us." She gave Mags a stern glance. "We aren't the authorities."

"Oh, right." Mags frowned.

I laughed at the disappointment on her face. "Come on. Let's get a coffee from down the street while the copies are made."

We strolled down the sidewalk, Caper's leash held firmly in my hand, and then entered the coffee shop. Heads turned, then hands clapped as those inside rose to their feet.

I froze, widening my eyes. What was going on?

"Coffee is on the house, ladies," the barista said. "You're local heroes." She grinned and took our orders.

Wow. Word traveled fast. We'd only found the girls yesterday.

"I don't like this," Ann said as we chose a table. "This puts too much attention on us."

"I agree. It also puts CJ number two in jeopardy. She can't have been at the school and the mall at the same time." I drummed my fingers on the table, then sent Davis a text expressing our concerns.

He replied with an order to come see him at the station.

With coffees in hand, we picked up the fliers, tacking them in every window and light post between the copy shop and the police station. Folks were more than willing to have the fliers put up, and some volunteered to help us put them around town. One man offered to take some to the next city. My heart overflowed with love for these people.

"Why are you crying?" Mags arched a brow as we entered the police station.

"Happy tears. I love these people. I love this town."

"You're a strange bird, CJ."

The receptionist ushered us immediately to the conference room where Davis joined us a few minutes later. "All right, ladies. I don't like all this attention on you." He speared each of us with a glance. "The agent acting as the high school version of CJ didn't show this morning."

"Because by finding the girls, we gave her away," I said.

"She knew the risk." Agent Tyson joined us and took a seat. "She would've agreed with us that finding those girls took precedence."

"What's her name? Her real name." I squared my shoulders. The agent deserved for us to know her true identity.

"Agent Silverman." His face fell. "Although we haven't found a body, we don't believe she's still alive. Tragic. She was a good agent."

"Have you been to my house?" Ann asked.

He nodded. "Signs of a struggle. I doubt the two young men confronted her. She could have easily taken them on."

Which meant the big guys had arrived. If we didn't find the young idiots, the others would. They wouldn't be nice about the betrayal either. "Those boys are in danger."

"No more so than if they were behind bars," Davis said. "They're goners either way. All they can hope for is to help us catch those in charge, get a lighter sentence, and protective custody in prison. Which is too good for them in my opinion."

"They're still human and don't deserve to die a brutal death. According to Ashley, they didn't, you know—"

"But they were going to sell the girls." Ann tilted her head.

"That does seem to be their intention." I glanced at Davis, then Agent Tyson. The boys tried to be some of the big boys and failed. "Now what?"

The look on his face told me I wasn't going to like what he was about to say. "You're going home and staying there. Let the townspeople distribute those fliers. No more wandering around town. The target on all three of your backs has grown too big to handle. If I thought you'd listen, I'd send you away somewhere until this was all over."

"At least you aren't doing that." I crossed my arms. "I'm no safer at home than I am on the street."

"You aren't helping your case, CJ. As for you, Mags, Milton will be sleeping on your sofa." He held up a hand to ward off her protest. "I know Larry is capable, but he isn't law enforcement."

"This is ridiculous." I shook my head. "I'll put Roy in charge of Heavenly Acres, and we'll all move in my Grams's house so we can be under one roof. What about Eric?"

"It's time to stop roaming the mountain for a while. Staying at the house is a good idea." Davis pushed to his feet. "Effective immediately. Go home, pack, and lock yourselves away." He hurried from the room to stop any argument.

"Good luck." Agent Tyson followed Davis.

"So, we're to be prisoners." Mags glowered. "How are we going to help these girls if we're locked away?"

"We'll make do," Ann said.

"I'm telling you right now if another girl from this town goes missing, I'm hitting the streets again." I yanked open my car door. "Their safety depends on every available person on the lookout."

"I agree, but if we can stay safely out of the way, we will. We can't help anyone if we're dead." Ann met my gaze over the hood of the car. "You know Eric will agree once he finds out that Agent Silverman is missing."

Yep. My husband would tie me up if he had to, but I also knew he'd go as stir crazy as I would if we were locked up for long. I eyed Mags in the backseat. I loved her, but living with her would be difficult. Two dogs, two cats, three men, and three women would pack Grams's little house to the max.

I laughed. "Since I'm the only married woman, looks like Larry and Milton share a room and you and Mags share the other one."

Ann paled. "Lord, help me not to strangle her."

When we arrived home, I filled Roy in on his new responsibilities. "You can handle things since you did a fine job for a week while we were in Maui."

He nodded. "As long as you are safely out of the way, I can do anything."

Such a sweet man. "Thank you. We'll be leaving shortly after Eric returns."

"Are you going to tell the other residents?"

"No. It's best we slip away. If anyone asks, just

say we took a vacation. You can reach me by my cell phone."

"Be careful, CJ. The world is a better place with you in it."

Smiling, I headed home, doused in the love of friends. I glanced at Mrs. Wentworth who watched from her tiny porch. When she caught my glimpse, she slipped inside. One of these days I'd find out why she disliked me so much.

"Davis called me," Eric said in response as to why he was home so early. "I've started packing."

I studied his face. "You're okay with this?"

"No, but we've had to stay there before. We'll survive it again." He pressed his forehead against mine. "It's for the best."

"I thought you'd say we need to run."

"That's what I'd like to do, but I know my girl too well to suggest such a thing. I'd like to take you up the mountain, deep in the woods, just you and me and live like hermits."

"Sounds wonderful. Maybe for a weekend after this is all over?" I cupped his cheek. "I can't run, Eric. I'm good at this."

"I know, baby. Let's finish packing and come up with a plan that doesn't end with us in jail or dead."

Chapter Fifteen

I entered Grams's house and choked back tears. Signs of a struggle were putting things mildly. Dining room chairs overturned, a crystal decanter shattered on the linoleum floor, and a stain on the rug that looked suspiciously like blood.

Mags clapped a hand on my shoulder. "We'll have things to rights in no time."

I nodded, swallowing hard. "I'm not sure how to remove blood from the carpet."

"I'll work on that. You sweep up the glass."

"I'll set the chairs back on their feet." Eric gave me a sad smile. "Larry will join us in a bit. He's hiring a firm to up the security on this place, so we won't be caught off guard like the agent was."

"Where do you want the bags?" Milton asked.

Directing him to the proper rooms was easy. Cleaning up one of the vases my grandmother cherished wasn't. The tears fell as I swept the pieces into the dustpan.

"Come on." Eric took the broom from me and led

me to the deck on the back of the house. "Sit. Mags is making tea. Soak in the beauty of the woods and let the rest go for a little while."

I lowered myself into an Adirondack chair and laid my head back. I'd have been angry to see the house I shared with Eric in such disarray, but to see my grandmother's like that, to know that someone pretending to be me had been taken and possibly killed, hurt. A lot. This house had always been my safe place.

"Here you go." Mags carried out a tray with glasses of tea. "Should we gather out here to come up with a plan?" She glanced at the woods. "Those trees make good hiding places."

"No one will get close without Hershey letting us know." Eric patted his dog's head. "We're safe enough for now." Once everyone joined us, he continued, "Larry will have a perimeter set up, similar to what we have at Heavenly Acres. We'll be able to watch the camera feed on our laptops. He's fairly certain not even a sniper could sneak onto the property before we see them."

"Fairly certain?" Ann tilted her head. "I want one hundred percent."

I did too, to be honest. "So, we're going to hide in this house and stare at our laptops all day?" I sat up as two men, accompanied by my uncle, strolled past the house pulling a cartful of equipment.

"For now." Milton leaned against the deck railing. "Ann and I are here to protect the rest of you nosy folks. If we keep you out of the way of authorities, they might be able to catch those guys."

"It was we women that found the girls." I

narrowed my eyes over the rim of my glass. "Don't shove us aside as useless."

"Sheer luck."

"Instinct." Mags looked like she wanted to punch him. "You either have it or you don't."

Milton shrugged. "Guess I'm lacking."

"Your flippant attitude is unbecoming, even for you." Mags narrowed her eyes in his direction.

"Can we return to the task at hand?" I glanced from Mags to Milton, wanting to defuse a rapidly escalating situation. We hadn't been crammed together for twenty-four hours yet and already two of us were butting heads. "So, we're installing security. That helps us. What are we going to do to stop the trafficking ring?"

"Milton and I are going to visit some truck stops," Larry said, joining us on the porch. "We'll pretend to be drivers and nose around. Hopefully, someone will approach us about some lovely ladies wanting company."

"That could be dangerous." I glanced his way.

"Yep, but I'm not as well-known as you and Mags. Neither is Milton. It might work. I've already run the idea by Davis, and he's in agreement. I've also rented a truck." Obviously having been an MP in the military worked in my uncle's favor.

"I'm not going to like staying behind." I crossed my arms. "If you find some girls, they'll want a woman to talk to. They won't trust men. Let me disguise myself as a young man." I glanced at my husband, waiting for him to tell me no.

He sighed and rubbed his hands down his face. "I don't want you immersing yourself into something that seedy. I'll go."

"But, the bad guys will recognize you."

"Not out of uniform, I bet." His smile looked forced. "I know that doesn't ease your concern about a female not being there, but you're too recognizable, CJ."

I didn't like being left out of the action. Not one little bit. "When are you going?"

"Tonight," Larry said.

Mags and I cut a sideways glance at each other. Good. She was thinking the same thing. We'd follow the men and do our own searching dressed as men. Our only drawback was the fact we wouldn't have an eighteen-wheeler. A problem that needed a solution.

"Who wants lunch?" I got to my feet. "The womenfolk can prepare sandwiches."

Thankfully, my two friends could take a hint and followed me into the kitchen. "What's up?" Ann asked. "You have that look."

"I need a semi." I grinned and quietly explained my plan.

"I know where we can get one," she said. "It's not usual for three men to drive the same truck, though. Normally just one, maybe two."

"Then one of us will stay in the back of the cab," Mags said. "Strap down your chest and put on a jacket, girlie, because you need to look like a trucker and not an Amazon. CJ can look like a young man easy enough. She's as thin as a twig."

"You're staying in the back." I glowered. Sure, I didn't have Ann's curves, but it wasn't necessary to point out the fact. A pair of overalls would hide what little I did have easy enough, and the pair Grams used to wear to garden still hung in her closet.

"This is insane," Ann said, "but I'm with you. I'm not staying at the house when lives could be saved by sticking our necks out. I'm willing to take the risk."

"So am I."

"Me, too," Mags said. "Where are you getting us a truck, and when did you learn how to drive one?"

Ann smiled. "A PI has their secrets and knows people in influential places."

The rest of the day passed slowly with far too much television watching and snack eating. As the men left, warning us to stay put, I turned on a True Crime show. Since they all knew I was a true crime junky, it ought to put them off the fact we'd be only minutes behind them.

The moment the men pulled out of the driveway, the three of us split and raced to put on our disguises. Ten minutes later, we set the alarm on the house and sped toward a lot where Ann said she could pick up the truck.

Another ten minutes later, I stared at the screen of my phone, searching for Eric's location. "Take the next exit."

Ann turned the wheel and downshifted, pulling into a crowded truck stop. "It would help if we knew which truck the guys were in. We'll be stopped before we begin if we end up parking next to them."

"Park over there." Mags pointed over Ann's shoulder to an area not as full of vehicles. "What do we do now?"

"We wait and see if a girl comes to us." Ann parked and cut the engine.

"That's it?"

"That's it."

"Shouldn't we be out looking for them?" I asked.

"Nope." Ann pulled her cap low and settled back in her seat. "Pretend to sleep. Act like you're on a stakeout."

I was horrible at stakeouts but copied her slouch and slid down in my seat. "What if someone does come?"

"We invite her inside and get her the heck away from here. Only one will come. That's all we'll be able to help today. Once we have her, we'll have to leave before we're discovered."

Hope dropped like a weight. Still, one girl saved was better than none.

"I have to use the restroom," Mags said from the back. "Let me out."

"No." Ann shook her head. "Milton or Larry might see you."

"You expect me to hold it until we get home?"

"Yes."

I chuckled as Mags grumbled and settled back into place. Mags didn't need to use the facilities. She wanted to nose around.

Movement outside the truck window drew my attention.

A young girl in shorts and a tank top approached the truck. "Want some company?" She posed and smiled.

Ann nodded and said in a low voice, "Sure. Climb in."

I shoved open my door, almost gagging on the odor of cheap perfume and sweat. The poor thing didn't look older than fifteen. I motioned my head for her to climb in the back.

"What is this?" The girl froze when she saw Mags. "It's going to be expensive for three."

"No need, sweetheart." Ann fired up the engine. "We're taking you away from here. You're safe with us"

The girl scrambled for the door. "You're going to get me killed."

I whipped off my hat, letting my hair tumble around my shoulders. "We're trying to stop girls like you from being exploited. Will you let us? What's your name?"

The girl broke into tears. "Melissa. My friend is still out there."

I glanced at Ann. "Can you go with Melissa to get her friend?"

"Where is she?"

"A few trucks over. Please?" Melissa raised imploring eyes. "We've been together since day one. I can't leave her behind."

Ann groaned and slid from the truck. "Make it quick. We can't be discovered."

Melissa followed Ann out her door and led the way. I kept my gaze glued on them for as long as I could until a knock on my window startled me. I yelped and jumped back, staring into the stern face of my husband.

Uh-oh. "Hello." I pasted on my most beguiling smile.

"Don't you ever listen?" His eyes flashed.

"We've saved another one, and she's leading Ann to her friend." I hitched my chin, refusing to feel guilty.

A few minutes later, Ann returned with two girls in tow. "The friend was at Larry's truck. We've been busted—oh, hey, Eric."

"Right. Meet us at the station." He marched away, leaving the girls to ride with us. My sweetie was rarely angry with me, but his emotions showed in the rigid lines of his back. I'd have a lot of making amends to do.

This was probably the first time two semis pulled into the parking lot of the police station. A stern-faced Davis met us outside, most likely informed by Milton what had transpired. I braced myself for a lecture.

"Come on, girls. He only looks mean." I shoved open my door and hopped to the ground. "Got two more, Detective."

"Do you care anything for living another year, CJ?" He frowned. "Get them inside quickly. You couldn't be more conspicuous, bringing those semis here. Talk about easy to follow."

We ushered the girls inside, stood stoically while Davis gave us a lecture on the stupidity of disobeying orders, then left the girls in the capable hands of Davis before returning outside so we could return the semis. Two more girls saved. Maybe I should change careers and become a professional rescuer.

Eric put his arm around my waist and hurried me across the parking lot. "Try to make it home safely, okay? Before you drive me completely insane." He kissed me and jogged to where Larry and Milton waited.

We returned the truck to its lot, then climbed into

Ann's car. "A job well done!" I held up my hand for high fives.

"We make a good team," Mags said.

Ann laughed. "It was worth the lecture from Davis."

"He's lost his touch. I remember when his lectures used to make me nervous." I clicked my seatbelt into place as my windshield shattered. With a shriek, I ducked. "Is someone shooting at us?"

"Yes. We've been followed." Ann pressed the gas pedal hard enough to press me against the backseat.

"Don't go home," Mags said.

"I'm not stupid." Ann yanked the wheel, hurtling us from the lot and onto the highway.

A vehicle behind us turned on its lights and raced after us.

"Don't look now, but there's a man hanging out of the passenger window and aiming a gun at us." Mags slouched in her seat. "I wish we had a rifle instead of that baby handgun Ann carries."

"My gun is just fine. What we need is someone to shoot for me. Unfortunately, CJ hates guns, and you're more likely to shoot one of us. Hold on, ladies, we'll have to make a run for it." Ann increased our speed, rocketing us away.

Chapter Sixteen

"**Have you noticed** that we participate in car chases far too often?" Mags said, staying low in her seat. "While exciting, I'm getting too old for this."

I was twenty years younger and never had enjoyed being chased by people with guns. "Where are we going?"

"Home if I can ditch our tail. If not, we'll be driving for a while." Ann leaned forward, eyes on the stretch of interstate ahead of us. "One of you should probably let the men know of our circumstances. They might find a way to help us."

I sent a rather jumbled text due to the speed we traveled at and the bumps in the road but hoped Eric could make out what I tried to say. With his GPS, he should be able to pinpoint our location and send help.

A bullet pinged the back of the car. Ann muttered something not very nice. She did love her big boat of a Chevy. "Do they realize how hard it is to fix a vintage automobile?"

"Don't think they care." I glanced at the jacked-up truck following us. "Maybe you could do something to make that truck flip. It can't take turns well, can it?"

"Worth a try." Ann whipped the steering wheel to the left, across the grassy median, and in the opposite direction.

The truck followed, teetered, and fell back to all four tires. Ann switched directions again. Horns blared as she took us straight into traffic.

"We're going to cause an accident. Come up with a new plan." I clutched the handle to the right of my head and thanked God for seatbelts even though mine had tightened during our mad dash.

"Stay straight," Mags said from the back, "or I'm going to lose my dinner. This isn't a carnival ride, you know."

"I need the two of you to stop harping at me." Sweat glistened on Ann's brow. "I'm doing my best."

My phone vibrated. I glanced at the screen. Relief flooded through me. "Eric said Davis is sending some squad cars to head off those in the truck so we can get away."

"I hope they make it quick. I'm almost out of gas."

"What?" My voice squeaked.

Ann shrugged. "I forgot to get gas in my haste to follow the men to the truck stop."

I leaned over to see the blinking red light. "How much do you have?"

"Not enough. I need to find a place for us to hide."

"The woods are dark enough," Mags said. "Pull

off. The goons in the truck will see the car but so will Davis. We just have to stay alive until help comes. And staying in this car lessens our chances."

"I agree."

"Okay. The second I stop this car, get out and run." Ann pulled onto the shoulder.

In unison, we shoved open our doors and darted for the trees. A barbed-wire fence stopped us a few feet in.

Ann stepped on one strand and pulled up on another. "Quick."

I scuttled through, followed by Mags, then did the same for Ann. With her size, the barbs snagged her shirt, tearing off a piece. I pocketed the fabric. No sense helping those following us by leaving breadcrumbs.

The moon filtered through the tree branches but not enough to make our path clear. The trees stood like dark soldiers around us, their whispers filling the air and sending shivers down my spine. I wasn't one to be afraid of the dark, but the spring evening left me with the strange feeling that a hungry witch waited for us over the next hill.

When we topped the rise, I was actually surprised not to see a cottage made out of treats. "Can you see the men?"

"No," Ann said. "Not knowing where they are is worse than spotting them. If they're hunters and trackers, we won't be able to get away."

"We only need to hide until help arrives." Mags leaned against a tree, her breath coming in pants. "Go on. Don't wait for me."

"We aren't going to separate." I frowned. "No

woman left behind and all that."

Ann spurred us forward. "If we can circle around and locate the car, we might be able to drive off before the bad guys find out. If we can buy some gas." She sighed.

"I like that plan. As long as we don't run right into them." My eyes had adjusted to the dark, but not well enough to go against someone who knew how to maneuver through the woods. A gunshot could ring out, striking one of us before we knew what happened.

"Follow me." With her gun at the ready, Ann led us to the right, making a wide circle.

I really hoped we were headed in the right direction. Sirens wailed in the distance. "Head for the sound."

"How can you tell which way the sound is coming from?" Ann stopped. "Nothing is the same out here."

A text came from Eric asking where we were. I replied we were in the woods.

What?

Trying to stay ahead of the bad guys until help arrives. We couldn't stay on the road.

How are we supposed to find you out there?

"Turn that off," Ann told me. "The light will give us away."

"Okay." I told Eric I had to go and slipped my phone back in my pocket. "My husband didn't seem happy that we're out here." I felt like we'd been walking for hours. We were probably going in circles. I fully expected our pursuers to show up at any time.

"I don't want to die dressed like an old man." Mags bent over and took a deep breath. "But if we don't stop soon, I'm going to have a heart attack."

"We can't stop." Ann took Mags by the arm. "Come on. We have to find Davis and the others."

A bullet kicked up the leaves at our feet, spurring all three of us into a run. Ann turned to return fire but didn't shoot.

"I can't see anyone. Stay behind a tree as much as possible." She plastered her back against a large pine tree. "Go from tree to tree as fast as you can."

"Nothing like a possible bullet in the back to make you forget how tired you are." Mags darted for another tree.

"Listen." The sound of cars on the interstate was the sweetest thing I'd heard in a long time. "This way." I bolted in the direction of traffic, coming up against the barbed wire fence again. "We did it."

We squeezed through the fence and made our way to the road. I couldn't see the car, the truck, or any police vehicles. How far had we run?

"This way." Ann headed to our left.

"How do you know?"

"Mile marker. I paid attention. We're about a mile away from our vehicle. We need to be fast before those men figure out where we've gone."

"Sounds good to me." Mags followed close behind Ann, leaving me feeling vulnerable in the back.

Wait a minute. I stopped and stuck out my thumb. "We can hitch a ride to our car. Those after us won't suspect it."

A beat-up Ford slowed. "Hop in the back," the

man said. "Where you headed?"

"Just down the road. Our car ran out of gas." I scrambled into the back and held out a hand to help Mags.

A few minutes later, the Good Samaritan dropped us off by our car, along with two police vehicles and the jacked-up truck. "I've a gas can in the back," he said. "It's got a couple of gallons. Enough to get you to a station."

"You're a prince among men," Mags said, handing me the can.

I passed it to Ann who put it in the car, then set it back in the truck bed. "Thank you."

"Not a problem."

The man drove off and we climbed back into the car. I couldn't be happier to be headed away from the big truck and sent Eric a text that we were driving to the nearest gas station.

Wait there for me.

Gladly. I glared at Ann. "No more letting your car go below at least a quarter of a tank. We could have died because of that oversight."

She grinned. "We're breathing for another day."

Fifteen minutes later, we had a full tank of gas and waited inside the gas station store for the men to arrive. Both squad cars pulled in front of the station, and Davis and Eric exited one of them.

Eric rushed inside and gathered me into his arms. "You scare me on a daily basis." His chin rested on top of my head.

"I often scare myself." I hugged him tight. "Can we go home now?"

"Follow the other squad car," Davis said. "Eric

and I will be right behind you. We'll talk when you three are safely home."

Even sandwiched between the two police cars, the tension didn't leave my shoulders until we pulled into the driveway of Grams's house. Larry stood from where he'd waited on the front porch, a rifle in his arms.

"You okay, love?" His gaze rested on Mags.

"I'm just fine." She caressed his face on her way. "I think we all need coffee."

"Already made." He grinned.

"My hero." She entered the house, the rest of us following. "Any visitors?"

"Quiet as a church on Monday," he said. "Not the same for you three ladies."

"Nope." I collapsed onto the sofa.

Davis stared down at me for several seconds before speaking. "Did you catch a look at those chasing you?"

I shook my head. "Not even sure if they were men or women, although I'm assuming men."

"Why did you leave the safety of the vehicle?"

"My fault." Ann pulled up a kitchen chair. "Ran out of gas."

He blinked several times. "Rookie mistake."

"Made a few of those this time." Her shoulders slouched. "So, we ran into the woods, circled back, hitched a ride from a nice man who had some gas to spare, and here we are."

"Lucky you." His features hardened. "Do I need to replace you, Lowery? You're supposed to be protecting these women, not going along with their shenanigans."

"Hey." I straightened. "We saved two more girls tonight."

"And almost got yourself killed."

I crossed my arms. "It would be worth it if it meant saving innocent lives. I know what I'm getting into. Those poor things don't. Isn't putting your life on the line what law enforcement does every day?"

"You aren't law enforcement."

I shrugged. "I've accomplished at least as much."

He looked ready to explode. "Leave the safety of this house one more time, and I'll put you behind bars."

"Promises, promises."

"Talk some sense into your wife, Drake."

Eric breathed deeply through his nose. "I've tried, but this time I'm on her side. Eight girls are free because of my wife's interference. Instead of badgering her, you ought to be using her."

I couldn't have loved my husband more than I did at that moment. "Use my instincts, Detective. Yes, I'll find myself in danger again, but we might just be able to stop this ring."

"The FBI will never agree."

"Then don't tell them." My phone vibrated. I read the text as an icy fist clenched my heart. "The ring's hit Heavenly Acres. Rose, Daisy, Amanda, and Dashenay are gone. Roy said the parents are waiting for us in the community center."

With no further questions, we raced for the cars.

Chapter Seventeen

We roared to a halt in front of the community center and poured from the cars. As one, we burst through the front doors and faced the stricken parents. Roy's pale face shone next to the teary one of his wife, Tammy. Dashenay's mother and Lucy stood off to the side with their arms around each other.

When they all started to talk at once, Davis held up his hands. "One at a time, please. Roy?"

Roy cleared his throat. "The kids were all hanging out at the playground. You know, like kids do. They were in a group, and Danny was with them. Three men came up and took the girls at gunpoint. Said they had some numbers to recoup."

My legs sagged. If Eric hadn't caught me, I'd have fallen. He lowered me into a chair while I continued to stare at Roy. The girls of my community were taken because I'd saved some other girls. Didn't seem quite fair to me to have these girls suffer because of what I'd done.

Davis turned his attention to Danny. "Son, mind telling me what happened?"

"The gunmen wore masks but were white, older, maybe around your age. I couldn't tell much. When I tried to stand between them and the girls, they pointed their guns at me and told the younger kids to run home."

That was something at least.

"They said they'd be in touch," Danny continued. "I got the feeling they wanted CJ. One of them cussed a lot."

Ice water filled my veins and I stood on shaky legs. "They want to trade?"

Danny shrugged. "They didn't say. Only that you'd be getting another message."

Another? I glanced at Davis. "I never received anything."

"Them taking the girls is the first message. Excuse me." He stepped outside, cell phone in hand, returning a few minutes later to inform us the FBI would be here soon to question Danny further. "As for the rest of you, there's nothing more you can do. Go home."

"Go home? How can we go home when the girls are missing?" I couldn't believe what I was hearing.

"Which is your fault, CJ." Lucy glared at me. "If you weren't always meddling in things—"

"That's enough." Eric's voice rose over the murmuring of the others. "CJ has saved girls. We'll find yours, too." He put his hand on the small of my back and guided me to the door. "Come on. We have work to do."

Back in the car, he turned to me, taking my hand

in his. "We will find them."

"You bet we will," Mags said, sliding into the backseat after Larry. "They'll come for you, we'll nab them, and find out where the girls are."

I liked the part about finding the girls but not the part about them coming after me. How many times could I face death and walk away?

After heading home and climbing into bed, sleep was a long time coming, but the exhaustion of the long day finally helped me drift off to sleep. Nightmares of the girls being shipped away where we couldn't find them had me tossing and turning.

Something had me captured, tied up. I bolted upright, stifling a scream, to find myself twisted in the sheet.

Eric put a hand on my back. "You okay?"

"Just dreaming." I peeled the sheet from around my legs and got out of bed. Grabbing my robe from a nearby chair, I put it on and headed for the kitchen and at least two cups of coffee.

We were a subdued group sitting around the table sipping the brew. "I want to go home," I said. "If they come, that's where they'll go."

"I'm sure they know about this place by now." Ann shook her head.

"But Larry fixed this house and yard up like Fort Knox." No one could get to me here. "Do you have a better suggestion?"

"I'm working on it."

"I say we wait until we hear from them again," Eric said. "Then we'll figure out our next step."

Waiting never came easy for me. While we sat around twiddling our thumbs, who knew what was happening to our girls? I took my coffee to the back deck and stared at the woods behind the house. I didn't think trouble would come from that direction. No, they'd wait for the moment I was alone and take me. The problem with that scenario was I was never alone.

Did I want to be? What could I do for Rose and the others if I were captured? Nothing. My fight had to come by not being taken. What should be my next step? Were the FBI questioning all my neighbors? Were they searching for clues? What vehicle had the girls been taken in? After forty-eight hours would they be lost to us forever? My head ached from all the questions I didn't have answers for. I turned as Caper and Hershey barked.

A few minutes later, Agent Tyson joined me on the deck. The grave look on his face alerted me that he came with bad news.

"We found Agent Silverman," he said.

"Where?" I held my breath.

"Sitting in a chair on the front porch of your home in Heavenly Acres. She'd been shot between the eyes."

I sagged against the deck railing. "Was there a message?"

He held out a sheet of paper.

I took it and read, "If you want the girls, you have five days to find them. Let's play a game. You need to follow the clues. Clue one…What a wild ride and chase through the woods that was!"

"I think this means where we pulled off the interstate." I glanced at the FBI agent's face.

"We agree but didn't find anything unusual when

we were there."

"I still need to look. These people will have left a clue only I would recognize." I headed into the house and out the front door before turning to face the others. "Well? Are you coming?" I realized they had no idea what was happening, but I didn't have time to explain. That would have to wait until we were in the car.

Everyone grabbed car keys, phones, and wallets, and followed me to the waiting cars. Agent Tyson nodded. "Follow me. Do not get separated. I can't believe I'm letting so many civilians escort me to a potential crime scene."

"It happens a lot with this group," Davis said. "Law enforcement is always teetering on the edge of what's allowed and what's frowned upon. Especially when it involves Miss Turley."

Guilty. "I've more than made up for any trouble by helping you bring down the bad guys." I opened the door to Eric's truck and slammed it shut behind me.

I was the first out of the vehicles when we pulled up, despite Eric telling me to wait until the area was declared safe. I only had five days, which meant I couldn't waste a minute of the time I had. I stood on the shoulder of the interstate and surveyed the thick woods. No, the clue wouldn't be in there. They'd make the hunt hard but not impossible. Those people wanted me to find them.

I turned my attention to the ground. "Everyone stay back. I don't want you to walk on the clue."

"Says the woman who disturbs crime scenes on a regular basis." Davis smirked.

"CJ." Eric put out a hand to stop me as I stepped into the grass.

"I'm not going far." Keeping my eyes at my feet, I headed one way, then turned to walk the other way, covering the area. I'd almost given up when something purple sparkled up from a thick patch of clover. "Aha." I picked up the sequined ribbon. "I found something like this near the girls we saved at the mall."

"Where is it now?" Agent Tyson held out a paper bag.

"Around my dog's neck." I shrugged at his frowning look. "I thought it was left behind from the department store. What do you think it is?"

"Part of a costume sewn for the girls to wear. We've found the site on the dark web where their photos are posted."

I dropped the ribbon into the bag. "So, if we find out who's making these costumes, we find the traffickers."

"In theory."

"This is the answer to clue one. Now, to find clue two." The mall or the local fabric shop? I chose the fabric shop, which wouldn't be open for another couple of hours. "Do you want the other ribbon?"

The agent shook his head. "It'll be no good to us now."

Knowing what it was used for, I didn't want it either. "Now what?"

"We wait for the fabric store to open. I'll meet you there at ten." He turned and strode back to his car, tossing over his shoulder for us to go home.

The minute we walked through the door, I

scooped up Caper and removed the purple ribbon from her neck. I started to throw it in the garbage before thinking better of it. I wasn't sure why I might need it, but I stuck it in a junk drawer anyway.

"Guess we can't make plans anymore," Mags said, taking a skillet from a cupboard. "We're being led by the nose, waiting for the next clue in a diabolical game. I might as well make omelets to give us strength."

"That sounds wonderful." I sat on the sofa next to Ann who opened her laptop. "What are you looking for?"

"The site Tyson mentioned. I've surfed the dark web before, so it shouldn't be too difficult. There." She turned the laptop so I could see. She flipped through the girls for sale. "I don't see any of the children from Heavenly Acres."

"Which means they aren't selling them yet." I heaved a sigh of relief. "Flip through again, slowly this time. Maybe there's something there to help us." As much as I hated looking at the photos, it needed to be done. We couldn't leave out any possible clues. "There." A girl wearing a short skirt, trimmed in purple sequined ribbon to match the tube top she wore. "The seamstress would be a woman, don't you think?"

"Most likely. Do you know of any locals that could be hired for this?"

"No." I slumped against the back of the sofa. "But then, I stay at Heavenly Acres most of the time, and don't know a lot of the townspeople. Mags?"

"No one comes to mind. First omelet is up, Larry."

"It would be someone close," he said, taking the plate from Mags. "Someone who could see what CJ was up to."

"Someone at the community?" I widened my eyes. "The only possible ones would be Mrs. Wentworth, the Smiths, and the Fosters." I remembered the shopping bags in Mrs. Wentworth's hands. My mind tried to see the logo on the bags, but I couldn't recall it. "We need to check out their rentals this afternoon. I'll say we're there for a routine maintenance check." I'd used the ruse before, and all leases mentioned that the checks would be done at random since doing so had helped in the past.

"Not without me," Davis said, accepting the second omelet.

"If you go with me, they'll know it isn't routine." I crossed my arms. "If you must go, stay out of sight. The residents are used to me going alone or with Mags tagging along." I glanced at Caper, thinking I should put the ribbon back on her collar so I could judge people's reaction. The thought of touching the purple sequins again made me shudder.

By the time everyone ate, we were running late to meet Tyson who paced the sidewalk when we arrived. He stopped, his gaze meeting mine. "Second clue is tacked to the window with other fliers."

Chapter Eighteen

We crowded against the window. Fliers covered most of the glass. Which one?

I saw everything from missing pets to babysitters for hire. "Maybe the shop owner will know something." I shoved open the door and approached the counter. "Can you tell me which flier was posted most recently?"

The middle-aged woman's brow furrowed. "That's a strange question."

"Do you recall selling this ribbon to anyone?" Tyson showed her the purple strip.

The woman pursed her lips. "I do carry that here, along with a wide array of other colors. Who are you people?"

He flashed his badge. "Think hard, ma'am. This is very important."

"Well, of course, I sold that. There's no other place in town to purchase sewing needs. Unfortunately, I can't tell you who I sold it to. Youngsters come in for that sort of thing all the time.

School plays, costumes, hair ribbons—"

"What about the flier?" I arched a brow. It had to have been tacked up within a day. Surely, she'd remember who put it there.

"The flier for tires was put up right before I closed yesterday by a young man."

"Can you describe him?" Tyson asked, pulling a small notepad from the inside pocket of his suit jacket.

"Thin, handsome, white. Wore a blue baseball cap. An older man waited outside, but I didn't see his face." Her eyes widened. "Is this about the missing girls?"

Tyson kept his face expressionless. I thought Ann had a great cop face, but this man had her beat.

I glanced at the white shopping bags on the counter, noted the navy-blue needle-and-thread logo, then moved back outside and found the flier for tires. I skimmed over it because it looked professional. Even I knew how to make a good-looking flier and shouldn't have discounted this. "These are very large tires."

"The kind truck drivers would need," Eric said.

"Why are these guys having me revisit all the places I foiled them up?"

"They're leaving a trail of breadcrumbs, knowing you won't be able to resist. I think they've studied you ever since we got involved in Maui."

I took a deep breath, trying to calm my escalating nerves. "I didn't ask for this."

"I know." His mouth quirked. "Trouble follows my girl. I agree that we couldn't have turned a blind eye to helping. Not after we knew what was happening." He held out his hand. "Let's put an end to this."

I slipped my hand in his and let him lead me to the car. My heart battled over wanting to stop the ring and knowing every step we took put us more in danger. My husband had my heart. I couldn't go on if something happened to him.

As if reading my thoughts, he leaned over and kissed me. "Stop worrying about me. You need your head on straight. I love you, Babe."

"I love you, too." I forced a smile. "Onward, sir."

Once we arrived at the truck stop, we congregated next to the building. "Where should we start looking?" I glanced at Davis, then Tyson.

"Let's start where your rented trucks were parked. Davis will go with the ladies, I'll go with the men. Yell if you find something." The agent motioned his head for the men to follow.

"Ann, lead the way," Davis said.

She did and we stopped to stare at the empty spot. "What are we supposed to see?" Mags frowned.

I shrugged. "Anything that doesn't belong, I guess." I shoved my hair out of my face, wishing I'd thought to bring a hair tie. Who invited the wind?

Papers rattled, blowing across the asphalt. If there had been a note close by, it would have blown away. I glanced from left to right, scoping out the area. Finding nothing, I moved to where the wind had sent blowing garbage against the building wall. I'd dug through worse, remembering the time I'd dove into a dumpster looking for a clue. I scooted things around with my foot. "Ann."

She and Mags rushed to my side as I held up a

dirty, wrinkled business card for a Chinese restaurant that no longer existed. "The only place you could get food from this place was the mall."

"So?" Mags tilted her head.

"Why would this card be here after all these years?" I grinned. "We're heading back to the mall."

Tyson agreed it was the best choice we had and led the way to where we'd found the girls. The store was empty. Same as the location of the Chinese restaurant. "Split up. Finding a clue in a place this big is going to take some time."

Tyson, Mags, and Larry went one way, while the rest of us chose to explore the upper level. "This is like the proverbial needle in a haystack," I said. "Why lead us to the restaurant only for it to be a dead end?"

"Maybe it isn't." Eric turned back. "Let's search it again. Whatever we're looking for will be subtle. The clues are going to get harder."

I agreed. The restaurant was more of a counter with a small kitchen in the back. We headed behind the counter and through the swinging stainless-steel doors. Dust covered every surface, proving the place had been vacant a long time. We should have brought the dogs. Caper had a talent for finding things.

Davis stood in the middle of the kitchen and turned in a slow circle. "Investigate anything not covered with dust."

"That narrows things down," Ann said, opening a cupboard.

I headed for the freezer at the far end, although I'd seen Tyson search it earlier. The door opened with a squeak. Using the flashlight on my cell phone,

I stepped into the darkness and slowly cast my light along the walls and then upward where a few hooks hung from the ceiling. One of them looked new and shiny.

"Hey, guys."

The other three joined me. "Why hang a new hook?"

Eric's brow wrinkled. "Wait a minute. There's a sporting-goods store, at least there was, called Hook, Line, and Sinker."

I grinned. "You have a marvelous brain, husband of mine."

We rushed to the sporting goods store. The steel gate was in place but not locked. Davis rolled it to the side and led the way into the cavernous space empty of everything except shelves and racks and gun cases.

"I'll check the restrooms," I said.

"Not without me." Ann followed. "I have a gun. You don't."

"Fine." I shoved open the door to the women's restroom.

"Here." Ann handed me a flashlight. "You'll wear down the battery on your phone and might need it."

"Thanks." I checked the stalls and found them empty. "Onto the men's." Also empty.

"Dressing rooms?"

I nodded. "Leave no stone unturned, they say." I shoved aside curtain after curtain. Something started clicking as I moved the last one and stared down at a young white man and his black partner. They were bound, gagged, and tied together with a bomb between them that had started counting down. I must have triggered it when moving the curtain. "Ann?"

"This is not good." She glanced over my shoulder. "I'm calling Tyson."

"We have less than an hour."

"*They* have less than an hour." She placed the call and explained the situation.

"Do you think they're the ones the first note meant when they said five days to save?" I'd hoped to find my girls.

"Possibly. Tyson said to leave the store immediately and wait for the bomb squad."

I locked eyes with the young men and reached for the duct tape over the blond one's mouth. "We'll get you out of here." I hoped I wasn't lying to them. They'd made a grave error in moral judgment but didn't deserve to die in such a way.

"Don't touch him. You might set off the bomb."

"I have to ask if they know where the girls are." I held my breath and slowly peeled the tape away. "Where are they holding the girls from Heavenly Acres?"

"We don't know. We didn't have anything to do with them. Help us." Fear shadowed his blue eyes.

"We're trying. Help is on the way."

Ann rushed me out of the store, collecting Davis and Eric on the way. "If it gets close to detonation time, we're out of here. Understand?"

I nodded and peered at Davis. "How good is our bomb squad?"

"We don't have one. We'll have to have one brought in unless the FBI has someone."

"There won't be enough time," my voice rose.

"Those boys will die."

"We'll have someone here in fifteen minutes," Tyson said. "We'll get them free."

Too close. "What about the next clue?" I darted back into the store, Eric on my heels. "Do you have a message for me?"

The blond nodded. "What you seek is closer than you know. Ten times two."

I glanced at Eric. "Mrs. Wentworth. She lives in house number twenty." Why make this clue so easy? Were they turning on her, too?

Now, I was torn between staying to see what happened here and confronting Mrs. Wentworth. "What has she done?"

The boy shrugged. "Something to anger them or they wouldn't be siccing the cops on her."

"Why not kill her themselves?"

"I don't know."

Back outside, I told the others what the boy had said. "We need to go."

Tyson pressed his lips together. "I need to stay. The rest of you are safer away from here. Either this place will blow in an hour or it won't. Good luck."

"The same to you." I really hoped he didn't die that day.

The rest of us raced for our vehicles. "We can't alert her that we're coming," I said. "Original plan?"

Davis nodded. "You and Ann will go to the woman's house. The rest of us will be close by." He gripped my shoulder. "Use your head."

"Of course." I gave him a shaky smile and climbed into the car with Ann and Eric.

Back home, the others hid behind number

twenty-one while Ann and I approached number twenty. Squaring my shoulders, I knocked three times and stepped back. "We don't fight her, Ann. I need to find out where the girls are."

"I agree. Just know, I'll come find you. Right along with your husband."

I smiled. More than one person had my back. I slipped my cell phone into my bra and waited.

"What now?" Mrs. Wentworth answered the door and narrowed her eyes.

"Routine inspection." I forced a smile. "We'll need to come in."

"I'm busy."

"My apologies." I pushed past her and headed for the locked bedroom. "Please open this door."

"You aren't here to inspect anything, are you?"

"Yes, ma'am, I am. Our handyman has been in this house several times, and this door is always locked. I need to make sure nothing needs maintenance." I met her glare.

Ann's hand hovered near the gun on her hip as she nodded. "Please, ma'am."

Mrs. Wentworth rolled her eyes and pulled a key from her pocket. "You don't know what you're doing."

"I'm pretty sure I do." After the key turned in the lock, I shoved open the door. Bolts of fabric were piled in a corner. A sewing machine sat on a small folding table. Yards of glittery ribbon hung from the wall. We found our seamstress.

I turned to face the woman. "How could you?"

"No crime in sewing?" The woman's face hardened as she pulled a gun from the pocket of her house dress and aimed it at my head. "Drop the gun, blondie. I won't hesitate to shoot."

Ann bent and placed the gun on the floor.

The older woman kicked it away. "I need you to trade for my life, Miss Turley. This tall thing with us is a bonus. Let's go."

Chapter Nineteen

As we stepped outside, an explosion came from the direction of town. My knees buckled. Agent Tyson and the boys.

"That, you foolish girl, is why I need you. I have no desire to be blown to bits." Mrs. Wentworth poked the gun at the back of my head. "Now, call off the watchdogs before I shoot you."

I met Eric's stoic but frightened gaze. We'd been in this situation before. His helplessness as he watched me be taken away.

"Put down the gun, ma'am," Davis reached for his.

"Who would you have me shoot first, Detective? The blonde or the brunette? Unless you want to choose, I suggest you lower your weapon."

Davis laid his gun on the grass, raised his hands, and took a step back. "You don't have to do this."

"Oh, but I do." She poked me again. "Your car, sweetie. Let the blonde drive while I keep my gun on you."

I mouthed, "I love you" to Eric and let myself be prodded toward the car. The only shining point about being captured was that I might see for myself how the girls fared. I'd rescue us all. I didn't know how, but between me and my Amazon friend, we'd find a way.

"You're awfully quiet for one who rarely shuts up," Mrs. Wentworth said, ordering me into the back seat.

"Nothing to say." I glared and climbed into the car, wanting very much to slam my elbow into the old woman's nose.

"Where to?" Ann glanced in the rearview mirror.

"South."

Ann sighed and drove past the men and onto the highway.

The silence in the car was so thick I fought not to hyperventilate. I might act brave, but I was far more frightened than I'd let this woman know. I wasn't stupid enough to believe they'd keep me around. What use would the traffickers have with a married woman when they had young girls? No, I'd be killed as an example, right along with Ann. The stupid woman sitting next to me was just as expendable. Without her sewing skills, they no longer needed her.

After about thirty minutes, Ann was told to turn right down a dirt road which took us to a dilapidated house. Several vehicles were parked out front, attesting to the fact the house was not vacant.

Two armed men stepped onto the sagging front porch and stared as the three of us exited the car. One of them stepped back into the house to be replaced by a third, clearly the leader. Handsome, hints of gray in his dark hair, expensive pants and shoes. He shook his head at the sight of us and strode in our direction.

"I've brought you a gift," Mrs. Wentworth said. Placing her hand in the middle of my back, she shoved me toward him.

"I see that. Two of them, actually. It doesn't undo your carelessness." He snapped his fingers at the man still waiting on the porch. "Take them inside." He removed the gun from Mrs. Wentworth's hand as we passed.

She looked appalled. "I'm part of this team."

"Not anymore. No one on my team is stupid enough to lose pieces of ribbon that led these dogs right to us."

I frowned. "I thought you wanted to be found. What about the game?"

"What game?" His voice deepened.

"That was *my* brainstorm," Mrs. Wentworth said, puffing out her chest. "Wasn't it fun? It brought you right to me."

I strongly suspected the woman might be losing her mind. "You blew up those boys."

"No, that was this man here." She squeezed past him.

"Inside, ladies." He gave us a mock bow.

I wasn't surprised to see Manu and Landon at the kitchen table. They grinned as Ann and I were shuffled down a hall. Things were looking more grim by the minute.

We were shoved into a room with bars on the windows and a locked door behind us. My heart leaped to see my girls, and I rushed to them, taking them into my arms.

"Why were you taken?" Tears sprang to Rose's eyes. "We were counting on you to save us."

"Don't give up yet. There are others looking for us." I removed my cell phone and searched for a hiding place. If it was taken from me, Eric wouldn't be able to track me.

"There's a loose floorboard over here." Dayshenay lifted a corner. "We were trying to dig our way out, but it's too rocky."

"You're a genius." I dropped my phone in before studying the room.

Two full beds took up most of the space. Paper plates and water bottles were piled in one corner. A closet held a bucket used as a toilet. I gritted my teeth against the way the girls were being treated but forced a smile to my face and rubbed my hands together. "Let's brainstorm a way out of here."

"There isn't a way," Rose said. "There's too many men with guns and a whole lot of woods out there."

"How many men?" Ann asked.

"Five."

"Well, there's more of us than there is of them." I hunted for something to use as a weapon. Anything sharp would do. We might be outnumbered, but I'd fight until the end. "All we have to do is last long enough for Eric and Detective Davis to find us." Which, hopefully, wouldn't take too long. I didn't know how much time we had.

A woman's cry of outrage came through the door seconds before Mrs. Wentworth was shoved into the room. She fell to the floor, landing hard on her hands and knees. She scrambled to her feet and rushed the door, only to have it slammed in her face. "I've given you everything!" The old woman pounded on the door. After a few minutes, she whirled and spit at me. "This is your fault."

"How in the world is this my fault?" I crossed my arms. "You willingly helped those men kidnap and sell young girls to the highest bidder."

She rushed me.

Ann held out her arm and clotheslined her, knocking Wentworth flat. "I suggest you find a corner to stay in before I hurt you."

The old woman glared from the floor. "I should have shot you."

"You might still get your chance." Ann grinned. "What does this ring want with CJ?"

She climbed to her feet and moved to the other side of the room. "I don't know. She won't be worth anything on the market."

"I heard them say they wanted to make an example out of CJ," Amanda said from where she sat on one of the beds. "They're going to put her on the web."

"What?" My heart dropped like a chunk of ice to my feet. Were they going to torture me and film it to keep others from getting in their way? I couldn't fathom the idea. Surely, they wouldn't.

The door opened and Landon stood there. "Come on, Miss Turley."

I was about to find out what my fate would be. "Mr. Landon?"

"It's actually Thompson." He grinned. "Mr. Barker would like to speak with you."

I squared my shoulders, pretending more bravado

than I felt, and followed him from the room and into an office.

"Please have a seat." Barker waved me into a chair mended with duct tape.

I sat. "You rang?"

He laughed. "Still spunky even with your future insecure. I like that. In fact, I've admired your tenacity."

"Get to the point. What are you going to do with me?"

"That depends on you." He steepled his fingers. "I could use a woman like you on my team. You look trustworthy. and not intimidated or frightened in the least."

"I shall decline." I clutched the arms of the chair to keep my hands from trembling. "Now what?"

"You and your friend will disappear. I won't get as much money from you as I will the girls, but there are people who will buy you for whatever reason they have. Most likely sport." He tilted his head. "Are you sure you won't reconsider my offer?"

"I'm sure." My fingers ached from gripping the armrest. What did he mean by sport?

"Then there's nothing more to say. Take her back to the room, Joe."

Landon, aka Thompson, gripped me by the arm and hauled me to my feet. "Foolish woman. Maybe I'll buy you myself and see how fast you run." He tossed me back in the room.

"What happened?" Ann asked.

"The boss, Barker, first asked me to join him. He said I'd be useful in nabbing girls." I sat on the edge of one of the beds. "When I refused, he said you and

I will still be sold, probably as sport. I'm not sure what that means."

"There are people who buy people to hunt them."

"Oh." He was right. I wouldn't last long. "We have to get out of here. I doubt we have much time." I dropped to my knees and glanced under the bed.

"What are you looking for?"

"Something to use as a weapon."

"We've looked," Dashenay said. "There's nothing."

"Aha." I held up a shard of glass I'd found stuck in the floorboards. "Anything sharp will do, girls. A nail, a piece of metal…"

That started a room-wide search. If we were all armed, we could attack when the next man entered.

"Here's the plan." I waved my arms for them to gather around, ignoring the snide comments coming from the old woman in the corner. "The next time someone enters this room, we toss the bucket on them, then attack. We don't have to kill, just disable."

"I'll grab his gun," Ann said, "which will even the odds a bit. They won't risk shooting you girls."

"Are you sure?" Rose arched a brow. "They can always find new ones."

"She's right." I glanced at Ann. "Can we chance it?"

"We have to. I don't think you and I will be here by nightfall."

"We'll be rescued by then." I held firm to the fact Eric would find me.

"Did you check to make sure your phone had service?" Ann tilted her head. "Don't you think if your phone was working Eric and Davis would have found us by now?"

"Oh." I got to my knees and retrieved my phone. "New plan. We force our way out of this room and make a run for it until we reach somewhere with service. Let them hunt us all."

"You're an idiot," Mrs. Wentworth said, laughing. "A group is far easier to find than a single person. Why not make a run for it yourself? Like you said, they won't harm the girls. They're worth a lot of money to them."

I glanced at Ann. "I'm not thinking clearly, but she's right. My brain is mush. Can we survive out there?"

"You must have learned something by being married to a park ranger." Ann gave a wry smile. "Why not make them an offer they can't refuse?"

"Are you nuts?" Rose looked wide-eyed from Ann to me. "You won't last an hour."

"Thanks for the vote of confidence." I gave each of the girls a hug. "Stay safe. Do whatever you have to in order to stay alive and well. We'll come back for you."

I nodded and knocked on the door. When Thompson answered, I said, "I have an offer for Mr. Barker."

"Come on." He motioned his head and led me back to the office. "Sir."

I stepped into the room. "Let's make a deal, Mr. Barker. Why should someone else have the fun of hunting me when you're the one I've caused so much trouble for?"

"What are you suggesting, Miss Turley?"

"You give me and Ann an hour head start, then come hunting. If we make it to the highway, we and the girls go free. Your men must be growing bored sitting around here."

He stared at me for a few seconds before his lips curved into a smile. "I'll make that deal only because you have no chance of winning." He held out his hand.

Fighting back a grimace, I returned his handshake. "We leave at dusk."

"Clever girl. The dark will give you an advantage."

I sure hoped so.

Chapter Twenty

I stood in front of the house with Ann as the sun slowly set over the mountain. Blood trickled down my leg. Refusing to show Barker I'd foolishly injured myself, I stood as straight as one of the pines towering over us, more than grateful that Mags wasn't with me on this part of the adventure. She'd never be able to make a run in the area that loomed before us.

"You're bleeding," Ann whispered.

"I stuck the shard of glass in my waistband." I shrugged. "I didn't want to be weaponless, and I forgot and bent over. It's minor. What do you have?"

"How have you stayed alive as long as you have?" She shook her head. "I have nothing. I'll grab a stick or a rock."

"By the grace of God." I gave a shaky grin and turned my attention to Barker exiting the house.

"You have a thirty-minute head start," he said. "That should be sufficient under the cover of darkness. Why prolong the inevitable?"

"The deal about the girls stills stands." I glared.

"Of course. I'm not completely without principles." He grinned. "I'd almost give up my dislike of nature to participate in the hunt, but alas, it will only be Thompson and my man, Smith."

Two against two. Much better odds.

"On the count of three, ladies. Oh, wait, you'll be joined by another."

Thompson pushed Mrs. Wentworth from the house. She fell to her knees with a shriek.

"Hopefully, she won't hold you back too much." He laughed. "One, two, three. Go!"

We darted into the protection of the trees. I pulled the glass from my waistband and cut off my left sleeve to protect my hand from getting cut. It took that long for the old woman to cover half the distance.

"Come on, CJ." Ann tugged at me.

"We can't leave her." I yanked free.

"She'll get us killed."

"Go, you fools." Mrs. Wentworth waved her arms. "I've earned my fate. Perhaps I still have a few tricks up my sleeve. I'm far too old to run."

Seeing the reason behind her words, I nodded and raced further into the woods. I hated leaving her behind, but the girls were more important to me than a woman who'd helped capture them. I'd mourn the loss of another life later. "Plan?" Since Ann had suggested this crazy idea, I really hoped she had one.

"Try not to get shot." She glanced at her watch, illuminating the face. "We have twenty-five more minutes. Run as far as we can, then hide."

"That's it?"

"Yes. Keep trying to get service on your phone."

I was getting tired of mad dashes through thick woods and actually wished for a car chase. Holding firm to my cotton-wrapped glass, I pressed on, following Ann's tall form further into the dark. The woman must have the eyes of a cat because she sprinted forward as if there weren't roots and low-hanging branches to trip her up.

"Don't slow down," Ann said over her shoulder. "I wouldn't put it past those men to have night goggles on when they come."

"Thanks for trying to cheer me up." I hadn't thought of goggles. If so, there'd be no place for us to hide. "What about a stream? Something we can jump into and have it sweep us away?"

"If I find one, that's a great idea." She glanced at her watch again. "Twenty more minutes."

I really didn't need an update every five minutes. "If they give us thirty-minutes, it'll take them at least fifteen, give or take, to catch up with us. That gives us forty-five."

"Okay, Pollyanna. When have these men played by the rules so far?" She held a branch aside to prevent it from slapping me in the face. "No more talking, just in case."

I wasn't heavy by any stretch of the imagination, but I was definitely out of shape. When Ann stopped to decide which direction to continue, I leaned against a tree to catch my breath. My thighs throbbed and my lungs burned, not to mention I'd kill for a glass of water.

"We need to find a place to hide." Without waiting to see if I was ready, Ann took off in a run again.

Surely we'd covered a couple of miles by now. Think, CJ. What are some things you've learned about the forest from Eric? "Hold up, Ann." I stopped and peered through the dark. A jumble of large boulders leaned against each other on top of thickly wooded rise. "There." I grabbed a bush and pulled myself up, using whatever would hold my weight to reach the top. Thank you, God, that I'd listened to my husband. If we sucked everything in, we could squeeze between the rocks. Please don't let there be spiders.

"This is great," Ann whispered. "A tight fit, but I doubt they'll think of us squeezing under some rocks that could fall and crush us at any moment."

"They won't." I took a chance and shined my cell phone over our head. It would take an earthquake to dislodge the boulders leaning against each other. "I have service, barely." I dialed Eric.

"Oh, thank God. Where are you, sweetheart?"

"Hiding on a mountain under a bunch of boulders. I don't know how much time I have. We can't be heard. We're being hunted. If we make it to the highway without being killed, the girls will be released."

"Whose crazy idea was that?"

"Ann's, but I went along with it."

"How close to the highway are you?"

"No idea. I think we're lost."

"We are lost," Ann said. "That's why we needed to find a hiding place. Cut the conversation short. We don't want those guys to hear us."

"Stay put," Eric said. "We have your coordinates

and will be coming. I promise to find you."

"What about Tyson?"

Eric sighed. "He's gone, along with the bomb tech and the two boys. Don't be one of them. I love you."

"I love you, too." I clicked off and perched on one of the smaller rocks. Waiting in the dark might actually be harder than running.

A twig snapped below us. I glanced at my phone. Cheaters. We were just now at the half-hour mark. Too afraid to move for fear of rustling the dead leaves under me, I held my breath and waited. Maybe it was a four-legged animal rather than the two-legged variety.

I held onto a thread of hope as no more sounds came. The thread broke. A whispered conversation drifted from below.

"If they make it to the highway," one of them said, "it'll be our heads Barker takes."

"Then we can't allow them to make it that far."

"Where are they?"

"I don't know, but if you don't stop talking, they'll know where we are." Another twig snapped.

I gripped Ann's hand.

She squeezed back and leaned forward to peer from a crack between two boulders. "They've moved on," she whispered. "We're safe for now. Can you pull up maps on your phone?"

No longer caring about spiders, I moved to the darkest corner of our hiding place and pulled up maps. "We're this far from the highway." I held my fingers apart about an inch before realizing she couldn't see me. "I have no idea how far away it is."

I held up my phone.

"Maybe half a mile."

"Should we chance it?" I asked.

She sighed. "I don't know. We're safe here for now, and Eric said they're coming."

"If they find us, can they shoot us?"

"I don't think they could fit. They might shoot off some wild rounds."

"Then, I suggest we stay." I lowered myself to the ground and prayed again for no spiders. I didn't know how long we sat there, but I'd fallen asleep and woke with a start as someone called my name. Was I dreaming or had help arrived?

Gunshots rang out in the distance. From where the cabin stood, I guessed. Approaching footsteps had me holding my breath until I thought I'd pass out. I clapped a hand over my mouth to stifle any noise I'd make releasing my bent-up breath.

A dog yipped. Caper! I scrambled from my hiding place. "Over here!"

Two men stepped from the thick foliage.

"It's Eric and Milton," Ann said. "They have the dogs with them."

I rushed into my husband's arms. "We're safe now."

"Not yet, sweetheart. The men hunting you are still out here. Thank your pup when you get a chance. She led us right to you." He took my hand. "Come on."

"I lost my weapon." I turned back.

"What was it?"

"A shard of glass."

"We've three guns among us. We don't need it."

He pulled me along after him. "We've a truck waiting a mile west of here. Davis and other officers have converged on the cabin where the girls are. All we have to do is make it out of here alive."

We took off at a run, stopping often for Eric to listen and study the area. Milton's heavy breathing sounded behind me. I glanced back to check on him, only for him to wave me forward.

"Maybe we should go slower," I told Eric. "Milton is struggling."

"He's fine. We can't stop." Eric led us on.

We continued to where Eric's truck was parked. All four tires had been slashed, spurring us back into the safety of the trees. Eric loved that truck. Unfortunately, since purchasing the vehicle, it always seemed to need repairs of some kind because of whatever trouble I'd gotten myself into.

Eric stopped in the middle of some thick brush and pulled me down. "We stay until we know where those men are. How many?"

"Two. Maybe they went back to the cabin."

"And maybe they didn't." He put a finger to his lips, then pointed across the clearing where the moon shone off the logo of one of the men's cap.

They were obviously waiting for us to return. Thank goodness they hadn't seen us approach the truck before hiding again. Well, I could be patient when the situation warranted. I'd sit there until the authorities found us if it took all night. Now that the girls were safe, and I had no doubt Davis had rescued them, I could sit tight as long as my man and my dog sat beside me.

"Let's shoot them and be done with it," Milton

said, hoarsely. He pulled a canteen off his shoulder and took a big swig.

I licked my lips, eyeing the canteen.

Eric thrust his into my hands. I took a big swallow, letting the water sit in my mouth before swallowing. I'd never tasted anything so good. Not knowing how long we'd be there, I put the cap back on and handed the canteen back.

A SWAT van roared up behind Eric's truck. I wanted to stand up and cheer as five men in armor poured from the back. A mad crashing in the bushes across from us alerted them as to where their target was, and as one, the team converged on the hunters.

We were safe. Once the two men were dragged to the van cuffed and cursing, we stepped from the bushes.

Davis peeked out from the van. "I'm glad to see luck is still on your side, Turley."

"The girls?"

"Taken to the hospital to be checked over, but they're fine."

"Mrs. Wentworth?"

"Dead. We found her buried in a shallow grave beside the house."

My shoulders sagged. So much death. "You rounded up the whole ring?"

"Barker and the rest." He clapped a hand on my shoulder. "You did good. Go home now and try to stay out of trouble for at least a year. I'm worn out."

I scooped Caper into my arms and followed Eric to the van.

At home, I gave Caper several treats, then collapsed on the sofa to snuggle against my husband.

"I want to have a baby."

"Now?" He chuckled.

"As soon as possible. A baby might be the only thing to keep me from sticking my nose where it doesn't belong."

"And give up all this excitement?" He arched a brow. "But, a baby sounds like a wonderful idea. Let's start now." He took me by the hand and led me upstairs.

The End

Dear Reader,

I hope you enjoyed this last exciting installment in the *Tiny House* series. It dealt with a more serious subject than the prior books, but the horror of sex trafficking is prevalent in our world today—in our communities, our truck stops, and our sporting events. Nearly 25 million people worldwide are enslaved against their will. Between 15,000 and 50,000 women and children are trafficked in the US every year. Learn more about this horrible thing preying on our women and children at Thorn.org.

If you enjoyed *Caper Finds a Treasure*, please leave a review on Amazon. Reviews are very valuable to authors.

God bless,
Cynthia Hickey

Enjoy the first chapter of *Secrets of Misty Hollow*

Prologue

Susan Reece's hand trembled as she touched the large envelope the detective slid across the desk. Her mouth dried, making speech impossible. She dropped the envelope into her purse and stood on shaking legs.

"I cannot stress enough the importance of never using your or your daughter's real names again. You wanted a remote location to live. Well, you've got one," the detective said, taut lines framing his mouth. "We can only pray it's enough to keep you safe. Here is a cell phone and the number to call when you arrive at your destination. We've transferred the phone into your new name, and it's paid up for six months. You'll have to find a job." He stood and held out a hand. "Good luck, ma'am."

She gave a quick shake of his hand and rushed from the room. Outside, she leaned against the wall and fought to control the tremble in her breath. What had she been thinking to leave a world that gave Kayla everything she needed and then some? Who leaves a life of luxury?

Still, Susan couldn't live that lifestyle anymore. Anthony would never give up looking for them. He wouldn't be pleased to lose his only child.

A semblance of control gained, she dashed to the parking garage and the Mercedes—a present she'd received after giving birth to Kayla. One more thing she'd have to leave behind. She stopped and listened for any sign she wasn't alone in the garage at ten p.m. Two cars sat there, hers and the detective's. She raced to the Mercedes and slid in, locking the door.

It took several tries for her fingers to grasp the key and start the engine. Time was of the essence. Not only did Susan need to pack what she could carry, but she needed to study the file in her purse. Her new identity. Her new home.

She parked behind the motel which had been home for the last few months and hurried into the tiny room she shared with her five-year-old daughter. "Thank you, Mrs. Johnson."

The old woman sniffed and nodded. "I don't approve of mothers running around at all hours of the night, leaving their children with virtual strangers."

"I didn't have a choice." Susan pulled articles of clothing from the dresser and tossed them, unfolded, into suitcases. A bus would be leaving the nearby stop in thirty minutes.

When she'd packed what little they possessed, she gently woke Kayla. "Come on, sweetheart. Time for the next part of our adventure."

"Are we going home now?"

"To a new home." Susan forced a smile. "We're going on a bus so we have to hurry." She handed her daughter the stuffed bunny she never went anywhere without. It was too precious to leave behind.

With a suitcase in each hand, Susan guided Kayla out the door and to the bus stop. Her skin prickled. Any second she expected one of Anthony's goons to pull up and order them into a car. The tension in her shoulders didn't ease until the bus stopped and opened its doors.

While Kayla curled up in her seat, using the bunny as a pillow, Susan finally opened the envelope in her purse. Driver's license, birth certificates, everything she need for a woman named Sharon Marshall and her daughter Karlie. They had a three-day journey to the small town of Misty Hollow, high in the Ozark Mountains. A credit card and a few hundred dollars in cash accompanied the important papers.

Susan sighed and stared out the window, tears streaming down her face. She'd done it. Left behind a corrupt lifestyle to start anew. It would work. It had to. She'd given up too much to fail now. The moment her head touched the seat back, her eyes closed.

When the bus stopped in Misty Hollow, Susan was more than ready to get off. The sign had stated the population to be 2300. "Stay close to me, Karlie. Remember, that is your name now. Can you do that for me?"

Karlie nodded, eyes wide. "There are a lot of trees, Mommy."

"Yes, isn't it wonderful?" Susan/Sharon felt like a fish flopping around. Being a city girl, she'd never been in a town this small or surrounded by so much green. The excitement bubbling up inside surprised her at being in a new place, starting a new life. Now to find someone who could take them to their new home. She pulled a slip of paper from her pocket and dialed the number. "This is Sharon Marshall."

"We'll have a local pick you up in less than ten minutes. Delete this number." Click.

They stood in the shade of a large tree until a rusty Ford pulled in front of them. "You the Marshall lady who bought the old Rogers cabin?" A grizzled man with a long beard peered at them through the driver side window.

Was she? "Yes?"

"Is that a question or an answer?"

"An answer?" She set the suitcases in the truck bed and helped Karlie climb into the cab. "How far away from town are we?"

"From here? About half an hour. From a town big enough to give you a taste of city life, you'd have to drive forty-five minutes in the other direction."

Her eyes widened. The detective hadn't been kidding when he told her she'd be living in a remote location.

Half an hour up the mountain, they pulled in front of a rustic cabin. A porch extended along the front of it. A truck that appeared to be in better shape than the one they rode in sat out front. At least they'd have some mode of transportation.

"It's a good place. Roof don't leak. Well water is fresh and clear. A garden plot already hoed out back with seeds planted. Old man Rogers had everything ready before keeling over. Good luck."

"Thank you." Susan retrieved their suitcases and headed for the house.

Obviously locking the door wasn't a common occurrence since the key was in the lock of the front door. "This is our new home, Karlie." She pushed open the door and stepped into a clean, comfortably furnished two-bedroom house.

Chapter One

"Bye, Mom." Karlie Marshall darted out the cabin door and rushed to her late model Toyota Tacoma. If she didn't hurry, she'd be late, again, for her shift as a waitress at Misty Hollow Diner. Her mom's words about being careful followed her across the yard.

Always the worrier, her mother. Quiet, content to work in her garden or fish the nearby lake, her mom stayed to herself, more than happy to sit at home when she wasn't working at the town's small library. Not Karlie. She loved her small town but wanted—no, needed—to visit a sprawling city. A place with more than the thirty thousand Shakerville had.

It almost wasn't worth the long drive just to buy something she couldn't find locally. Plus, whenever she mentioned leaving, her mother would almost have a heart attack. At twenty-five, it was past time for Karlie to make her own way. The problem was…she didn't know what she wanted. She loved Misty Hollow but craved a little more excitement than the small town had to offer.

The whoop whoop of a siren sounded behind her. Karlie glanced in her rearview mirror to see the blinking red and blue lights of a police car, then down at the speedometer. Ugh. Speeding again. She doubted she'd get away with a warning this time. She watched an officer approach in her side-view mirror. Not a familiar face. Was this the new sheriff everyone was talking about?

He tapped on the window. "License and registration, please."

Sighing, Karlie rolled down her window, then reached over to open the glove compartment. "I'm sorry, Sheriff. I was speeding. I'm late for work."

"Later now." His lips twitched. He took the documents and returned to his SUV.

Karlie leaned her head against the steering wheel. Idiot. She jerked upright as the sheriff returned. "You're new?"

"Sheriff Westbrook, at your service." He handed her back her documents, then a ticket.

"You're giving me a ticket?" Her voice rose.

"You were going fifteen miles over the speed limit, ma'am."

Her shoulders slumped. "Fine." She shoved the ticket into her purse. "Welcome to Misty Hollow." When he stepped back, she sped away, careful to only go five miles over the limit. She'd have to work overtime to pay for the ticket.

If she weren't so angry, and late, she'd dwell on how handsome the new sheriff was even with the reflective sunglasses he wore. Dark blond hair, chiseled chin with just a hint of a dimple. Too bad.

Darn. Her speed had crept up again.

She glanced in her rearview mirror. Was he following her? She slowed and took the turn into town.

"Sorry." She rushed to the back to put her purse in her locker. "I got pulled over for speeding."

"Bound to happen sooner or later with the way you drive." The owner, Myrtle McIlroy shook her head. "Maybe I should put you down for half an hour earlier every day so you'll arrive when you're actually supposed to."

Karlie laughed, then noticed her boss's new hair color. "Nice. Makes you look like Lucille Ball."

"Stop the flattery and get to work. We're already busy with the morning rush." She waved a dish towel in Karlie's direction. "The other girl called in sick. I've been busier than a one-armed paper hanger."

Karlie grabbed her apron and a menu as the bell over the diner door jingled. She rushed out and skid to a halt as the new sheriff entered. She swallowed when he smiled her way. "Just one?"

He nodded, removing his sunglasses to reveal hazel eyes. "Yes, ma'am."

"It's Karlie. Follow me, please." She led him to a booth. "I know cops like to be able to see all exits. Hope this will suffice."

"It will." He set his hat on the table and took his seat.

"Coffee?" Karlie handed him a menu.

"Please." The dimple in his cheek deepened. "Newspaper?"

She left and returned with both, her gaze landing on the front page. "Who's Anthony Bartelloni?" She motioned to the story of a man being released from prison.

"Mob boss. He was released on probation. Should have stayed locked up for a very long time. I'll have the breakfast special."

Karlie placed the order and hurried to serve another customer, then glanced at the paper. The article said that Bartelloni had skipped out of town, left New York for parts unknown. She'd never heard the name before, but mobs were dangerous, right? She'd read about them in books.

"Table four's up," Myrtle called.

Karlie placed another order and carried the sheriff's food to him. "Let me know if you need anything else."

"How do you like Misty Hollow?"

"It's okay. A bit boring, and everyone knows everything about everyone else. Gossip is the favorite pastime." She smiled. "You arrived a couple of days ago, right?"

He nodded. "Looking forward to a slower pace."

"I'd say you've been busy already. Who tickets people before nine a.m.?" She arched a brow over flashing blue eyes, her smile fading. "Enjoy your breakfast." She marched away.

~

Yes, Heath had been busy. He knew exactly who Karlie Marshall was. Also knew who she used to be. With Bartelloni's whereabouts unknown, Heath had been filled in on the possible danger to Karlie and her mother. The challenge would be keeping them safe without revealing their true identities. He was counting on the Misty Hollow gossip chain to let him know if any strangers arrived in town.

Karlie's laugh drew his attention to the pretty redhead. Imagine his surprise when he realized the identity of the woman he'd ticketed that morning. Heath hadn't expected to meet her so soon upon arriving in Misty Hollow. He'd been told that Sharon Marshall was a bit of a recluse and figured the daughter was as well.

Orders had been to make friends with the Marshall women. He wasn't off to a very good start. He read through the newspaper article. There wasn't much to go on. The FBI feared someone had leaked information about the women, but whether Bartelloni knew exactly where they were was unknown. So, erring on the side of caution, Heath went undercover as the new sheriff. He glanced out the window at the trees and vintage brick buildings. Staying here wouldn't be a hardship. It sure beat the concrete jungle of the city.

Breakfast finished, he left a hefty tip and headed to the register to pay for his meal and the paper. "Give the chef my compliments," he told Karlie.

"Myrtle, the sheriff said the food was good," she turned and called through the pass-thru window.

A middle-aged woman with bright orange hair popped up and grinned. "Thank you, Sheriff. Come again."

"I'll be a regular, most likely." He nodded and left, heading for his car. He'd been on the mountain to familiarize himself with the area around the Marshall home. Now, he intended to drive the other mountain roads to acquaint himself with empty places a man could hide. The area was so wooded sneaking up on a home would be easy.

His radio beeped. "Sheriff Westbrook."

"Sheriff, we've a call of a domestic situation on Coon Road," his receptionist, Annie, said.

"On my way." He punched the address into his GPS and sped toward the address.

A rundown trailer sat in the middle of what looked like a junkyard, but was more the result of hoarding. A pit bull barked and pulled against the chain holding him to a tree. Heath unclipped his gun holster, ready to shoot if the dog broke loose and charged. Loud voices came from inside the trailer. Heath beeped the horn and exited his SUV.

A man stepped onto a sagging porch. "What?"

"We've had a call about a disturbance."

"From who? We ain't got no neighbors." The man's stomach stretched the limits of a stained tee shirt.

"Is your wife home?"

"Sally, get your butt out here. The sheriff wants to talk to you."

A woman, as thin as the man was pudgy, joined him on the porch. "Shut up, Brute," she hollered at the dog. "I can't hear myself think." She crossed her arms. "What can I do for you, Sheriff?"

"Everything all right here?" He glanced from one to the other. Who'd called the sheriff's department? A hunter, maybe? The man was right. There were no neighbors within hearing distance.

"You might have to arrest me," she said. "I'm about to beat my husband's head in."

"Let's not do that. What's the problem?"

"She's mad because I sold some of her scrap metal to buy beer." The man rolled his eyes. "Look at this place. How'd she know anything was missing?"

How indeed? Heath warned them about keeping things civil and returned to his vehicle. If it had been a hunter who made the call, they were hunting illegally. His day just got busier. He drove down a little-used path called a road and parked next to Misty Hollow Lake. A red-haired woman fished from the bank. Sharon Marshall.

She turned as he cut off the engine. "Howdy, Sheriff."

"Ma'am. Did you place a call to the station about a disturbance?"

"Yes. They were disturbing the peace, and I feared someone would be injured." Worry crossed the woman who looked like an older version of Karlie.

"Just an argument. Getting any bites?"

She bent over and lifted a string from the water. "Three bass. Enough for supper."

He wanted to warn her not to go out alone. To stay home. But, without solid proof that Bartelloni knew where she was, making her afraid seemed wrong.

"Why don't you come by for supper?" She smiled. "There'll be plenty." She gave him her address. "It's always nice to make friends with the local authorities."

Smart woman. Making friends meant local law enforcement would keep a closer eye on their friend.

Would she change her mind when she heard he'd ticketed her daughter? "I'd love to. See you later, ma'am."

By the end of his workday, Heath looked forward to a home-cooked meal. Eating out became old after a while, and he wanted a chance to see the Marshalls in their home. Determine, if possible, how defenseless they might be.

He changed into jeans and a button-up shirt, shoved his feet into cowboy boots, packed his things and then checked out of the motel. He climbed into his SUV, radio clipped to his belt. He might be officially off work, but his job never really ended at five o'clock. Not in such a small town where the station held him and two others.

Heath pulled into the graveled drive of the Marshall place and studied the cleared lawn. As with most of the homes out of the town limits, woods surrounded the house on three sides. Someone had cleared a nice space for a lawn and a garden. But this place gave a new meaning to the word, remote. A good thing when in the Witness Protection program. Bad if someone you'd wronged wanted to get to you—

On the porch, he raised his hand to knock and stopped as Karlie's voice rose inside.

"Mom, why does the DNA test I got back today show that I'm the daughter of Anthony Bartelloni?"

Website at www.cynthiahickey.com

Multi-published and Amazon and ECPA Best-Selling author Cynthia Hickey has sold close to a million copies of her works since 2013. She has taught a Continuing Education class at the 2015 American Christian Fiction Writers conference, several small ACFW chapters and RWA chapters, and small writer retreats. She and her husband run the small press, Winged Publications, which includes some of the CBA's best well-known authors. She lives in Arizona and Arkansas, becoming a snowbird, with her husband and one dog. She has ten grandchildren who keep her busy and tell everyone they know that "Nana is a writer".

Connect with me on FaceBook
Twitter
Sign up for my newsletter and receive a free short story
www.cynthiahickey.com

Follow me on Amazon
And Bookbub
Enjoy other books by Cynthia Hickey

Brothers Steele
Sharp as Steele
Carved in Steele

Forged in Steele
Brothers Steele (All three in one)

The Brothers of Copper Pass
Wyatt's Warrant
Dirk's Defense
Stetson's Secret
Houston's Hope
Dallas's Dare
Seth's Sacrifice
Malcolm's Misunderstanding

Fantasy
Fate of the Faes
Shayna
Deema
Kasdeya

Time Travel
The Portal

Tiny House Mysteries
No Small Caper
Caper Goes Missing
Caper Finds a Clue
Caper's Dark Adventure
A Strange Game for Caper
Caper Steals Christmas

Wife for Hire – Private Investigators
Saving Sarah

Lesson for Lacey
Mission for Meghan
Long Way for Lainie
Aimed at Amy
Wife for Hire (all five in one)

A Hollywood Murder
Killer Pose, book 1
Killer Snapshot, book 2
Shoot to Kill, book 3
Kodak Kill Shot, book 4
To Snap a Killer
Hollywood Murder Mysteries

Shady Acres Mysteries
Beware the Orchids, book 1
Path to Nowhere
Poison Foliage
Poinsettia Madness
Deadly Greenhouse Gases
Vine Entrapment

CLEAN BUT GRITTY Romantic Suspense

Highland Springs

Murder Live
Say Bye to Mommy
To Breathe Again
Highland Springs Murders (all 3 in one)

Colors of Evil Series

Shades of Crimson
Coral Shadows

The Pretty Must Die Series

Ripped in Red, book 1
Pierced in Pink, book 2
Wounded in White, book 3
Worthy, The Complete Story

Lisa Paxton Mystery Series

Eenie Meenie Miny Mo
Jack Be Nimble
Hickory Dickory Dock

Secrets of Misty Hollow

Hearts of Courage
A Heart of Valor
The Game
Suspicious Minds
After the Storm
Local Betrayal

Overcoming Evil series
Mistaken Assassin
Captured Innocence
Mountain of Fear

Exposure at Sea
A Secret to Die for
Collision Course
Romantic Suspense of 5 books in 1

INSPIRATIONAL

Nosy Neighbor Series
Anything For A Mystery, Book 1
A Killer Plot, Book 2
Skin Care Can Be Murder, Book 3
Death By Baking, Book 4
Jogging Is Bad For Your Health, Book 5
Poison Bubbles, Book 6
A Good Party Can Kill You, Book 7 (Final)
Nosy Neighbor collection

Christmas with Stormi Nelson

The Summer Meadows Series
Fudge-Laced Felonies, Book 1
Candy-Coated Secrets, Book 2
Chocolate-Covered Crime, Book 3
Maui Macadamia Madness, Book 4
All four novels in one collection

The River Valley Mystery Series
Deadly Neighbors, Book 1
Advance Notice, Book 2
The Librarian's Last Chapter, Book 3
All three novels in one collection

Historical cozy
Hazel's Quest

Historical Romances
Runaway Sue
Taming the Sheriff
Sweet Apple Blossom
A Doctor's Agreement
A Lady Maid's Honor
A Touch of Sugar
Love Over Par
Heart of the Emerald
A Sketch of Gold
Her Lonely Heart

Finding Love the Harvey Girl Way
Cooking With Love
Guiding With Love
Serving With Love
Warring With Love
All 4 in 1

A Wild Horse Pass Novel
They Call Her Mrs. Sheriff, book 1 (A Western
Romance)

Finding Love in Disaster
The Rancher's Dilemma
The Teacher's Rescue

The Soldier's Redemption

Woman of courage Series

A Love For Delicious
Ruth's Redemption
Charity's Gold Rush
Mountain Redemption
Woman of Courage series (all four books)

Short Story Westerns
Desert Rose
Desert Lilly
Desert Belle
Desert Daisy
Flowers of the Desert 4 in 1

Contemporary

Romance in Paradise
Maui Magic
Sunset Kisses
Deep Sea Love
3 in 1

Finding a Way Home
Service of Love
Hillbilly Cinderella
Unraveling Love
I'd Rather Kiss My Horse

Christmas

Dear Jillian
Romancing the Fabulous Cooper Brothers
Handcarved Christmas
The Payback Bride
Curtain Calls and Christmas Wishes
Christmas Gold
A Christmas Stamp
Snowflake Kisses
Merry's Secret Santa
A Christmas Deception

The Red Hat's Club (Contemporary novellas)

Finally
Suddenly
Surprisingly
The Red Hat's Club 3 – in 1

Short Story

One Hour (A short story thriller)
Whisper Sweet Nothings (a Valentine short romance)

www.ingramcontent.com/pod-product-compliance
Lightning Source LLC
Chambersburg PA
CBHW070300120726
47910CB00007B/2327